the trouble with
♡ falling

Also by Rachel Morgan

RACHEL MORGAN

the trouble with

♥ falling

THE TROUBLE WITH FALLING

ISBN 978-0-9946953-8-3

RACHEL
MORGAN

THE GUY ON THE OTHER SIDE OF THE CRAFT SUPPLIES store is watching me. Perhaps it's because I've been sitting on the worn out carpet against the scrapbooking shelf for over an hour, slowly tapping my iPad. It isn't the kind of store floor one would normally get comfy on for several hours, so he no doubt thinks I'm a bit strange. The people who work here think I'm strange, but I've sat in this store every day after school for the past year, so they're used to me now. And as long as they don't bother to put any chairs out, I'll continue to use the floor.

I tilt my head down again, letting my hair fall forward to shield my face. Strands of unnaturally dark hair block at least half my view of the iPad, but I'm not doing anything that requires a great deal of skill, so it doesn't matter that I can't see the whole screen. The colouring book app requires me to do little more than tap sections of the drawing to automatically fill them with colour. It's the most boring app I've ever used, but after studying all night, my brain is happy with boring.

I fill in another few sections of colour before looking up again. Yep, the guy with the short hair and the mountain silhouette on his T-shirt is definitely watching me. Creep. No matter how strange he might think I am, he shouldn't be staring. It's rude. With a frown, I turn back to my iPad, hoping he'll grow bored and leave the store.

He doesn't.

After examining some of the brush pens—which reminds me that I need a new soft felt tip one—he wanders around a shelf and reaches my side of the store. "Is something wrong?" I ask loudly when I catch him looking my way again.

He turns to face me fully, a bright smile appearing on his face. "Uh … nothing huge. I noticed you're limiting your creativity, that's all."

"Excuse me?"

"That silly colouring book app," he explains, gesturing to my iPad. "Colouring is way more satisfying if you do it for real. On a real page, with real pencils and pens."

He's right, of course, but I'm not about to admit that to him after he's been so rude. *Creepy British stalker dude.* Without looking down, I slide my hand over the iPad, loosely covering the surface. "Digital colouring *is* real colouring."

"Oh, yes, I agree with you on that. But that's not what you're doing. You're just tapping a screen."

"And you're just butting rudely into someone else's business."

"No, sorry, I'm just … challenging you." He gives me an irritatingly large grin, as if that could possibly excuse his rudeness. "Getting you thinking. Starting a conversation."

"Maybe I don't want to start a conversation."

"Look, just try it." He grabs the pad of paper people use to test the pens on before they buy them. "You've got drawing utensils all around you, after all. Makes sense to use the real thing."

"No thanks. I'm happy with my 'silly colouring book app.'"

"Oh come on. It'll be quick." He scoops up a pen and some of the tester pencils. "I won't interrupt you for long."

"You've already interrupted me for too long." I pull my knees up and return my focus to my iPad. I know I'm the one being rude now, but I don't come to this store every day to make friends. I come here to work in silence while waiting for my lift because it's unsafe to walk from the bus stop all the way home.

Instead of being offended, the overly friendly guy holds the paper and pencils out towards me and says, "It's easy. You'll soon see how much more relaxed you feel from the act of real colouring in. Just draw some random squiggles for the outline, and then—"

"I don't want to draw random squiggles."

"Okay, well I can draw the random squiggles, and you can—"

"No thank you," I say, loudly this time. And fortunately,

3

at that moment, my phone chirps on the floor beside me. *Almost there*, says the message that lights up my phone's screen. "Look at that," I say, grabbing the phone, pushing my iPad into my bag, and standing. "The universe has excellent timing, don't you think?"

He places the notepad and pencils back where they came from. "If that was the universe texting you, then yes. It sure does."

I roll my eyes as I slide my phone into my shorts pocket and lift my bag onto my shoulder. "Idiot," I mutter.

"Seriously," the guy says. I hear his footsteps behind me as I walk past shelves lined with jars of paint. "Did the universe just text you?

"Oh my gosh, stop following me!"

"Because that's amazing. Can you give her my number? I'd love to get a text from—"

"Thank you *so* much," I say, swinging around to face him as I reach the door, "for ruining my last ever afternoon in this store."

A wall of heat slams into me as I tug the heavy glass door open. Without looking back, I let the door swing shut and walk away. I stride along the pavement, past the coffee shop with its fake Christmas tree in the window and the clothing boutique with Santa hats on all the mannequins. I stop at the corner where I always wait, lean against the stop sign pole, and pull my hair away from where it's begun to stick to the back of my neck. While wrapping a hairband around my messy ponytail, I realise I don't actually know which car I'm looking out for. In my haste to get away from the craft store weirdo—who has not followed me out here, I'm relieved to see—I didn't even look at who the 'Almost there' message was from. I remove my phone from my pocket to check if it was Dad, Mom or Sarah.

Sarah: Almost there.

I close the app and open Artster to see if Lex has posted anything new. He hasn't sent me any messages in the past day, but he has uploaded a watercolour of random rainbow clouds. Looks digital, though. Probably an app he was playing around on—an app that involves a small amount of skill, unlike the one I was just using. Smiling to myself, I tap through to the messages section of Artster.

AngelSH: Warning—I think a unicorn puked on your gallery. Might want to see to that.

Next, I open my email and skim through notifications from the various art sharing sites I belong to. I stop when I see 'Request for fantasy illustration' in one of the subject lines from a Mr A. T. Dawson. The email is short, simply asking how much it would cost for a detailed illustration of a castle on a lake with a stormy sky and a serpentine monster erupting from the water. I type a quick reply directing the enquirer to the pricing page and portfolio examples on my website and wonder yet again why people don't bother to look at this page before contacting me.

A loud hoot pulls my attention away from my phone. I

look up to find my sister's car stopping in front of me. After pushing my phone back into my pocket, I open the passenger door and slide inside. "Hey!" Sarah beams as excitedly as if she just won something. "Last day ever!"

"Hmm?"

"Of school," she adds. "Your last day of school."

"Oh. Yeah." I pull the seatbelt across my body and click the buckle into place.

"Seriously? That's all you've got? You're supposed to be *excited*, Soph."

"I am excited." I give her my best smile. "This is me being excited."

"Uh huh." She takes one last look at me before pulling away from the stop street. "At least you ditched the uniform already."

"Yes. See? I'm totally excited about school ending." I wipe away the sweat gathering along the top of my brow and lean forward to adjust the air vents on my side of the car. "I couldn't wait to get out of that horrible dress. I got changed straight after the exam."

"How was it?"

"Okay, I guess." It was Art History. One of the few exams that was actually better than okay. I didn't make much of an effort for any of my other subjects. "Is your aircon still broken?" I ask, holding my hand in front of one of the vents. "This air feels almost as hot as outside."

"Yes, sorry. I haven't had time to take the car in yet."

I flop back against my seat. "I hate summer in Durban."

"It does kinda drain one's energy." Sarah rolls her

window down a bit further.

"Yeah." I stare out of my window as we join the slow-moving Friday afternoon traffic. "Is the house full of people now?"

"Not yet. Julia and Josh's London flight was delayed, so they missed their connecting flight from Joburg and had to take a later one. Mom's going to fetch them after work. Caleb arrived this morning, but Aiden took him out somewhere for the day. Not sure where they are right now."

I look at her. "Which one's Caleb again?"

"Aiden's best man?" Sarah says, throwing a glance at me with eyebrows raised slightly, as if I should know this.

"Right, yeah."

"And that's it for now. Emily and Harry only arrive next week, and Aunt Maggie said they can stay with her."

Emily and Harry. Aiden's sister and brother-in-law. Those names I do remember.

"So we'll have eight people in the house, which isn't too bad," Sarah continues. "Jules and Josh will be in her old room, I'm in my old room, and Aiden and Caleb are sharing your old room."

"And I'll be hiding upstairs in the attic where no one can find me," I mutter.

"Right, and I'll probably be hiding there with you when all the social interaction becomes too much," Sarah says with a laugh. She lived in her own place up until the end of last month, a flat nearby that she rented with a friend from the magazine she works at. But with wedding expenses piling up, she moved back home at the beginning of the month. Aiden did pretty much the same thing with the room he was renting next to the university. Moved out and took up residence on a colleague's couch until this morning when his friend Caleb arrived. Now they'll both be taking up extra space and bathroom time at our house instead.

Wonderful.

I let my eyes slide shut until I feel the car turning right into Girvan Avenue. Sarah slows after we've passed a few houses and turns into the driveway of the only home I've ever known. I release the buckle of my seatbelt as the gate slides open and Sarah drives in. "Aaaaand that's it," she says as she cuts the ignition. "Last time I'll ever pick you up after school."

"Yeah," I say with a small smile. *I'm finally free.* Well, not entirely. I'm free of school and all the useless things I had to spend my time on there, but I won't be completely free until I'm out of here and on my own, travelling exotic countries and filling as much time as I can with my art. Until I can fund that dream, though, I'm stuck here at home.

"Want something to eat?" Sarah asks once we're inside.

"No thanks." Since no one else is here and I'm not yet forced to be friendly, I head straight for the attic. It isn't actually an attic, of course, but Dad started calling it that while it was being built, and the name stuck. It used to be Sarah's space, but I claimed it the moment she moved out. When we were growing up, she had a room downstairs like the rest of us, but some time after she quit university and came home to pursue writerly dreams, Mom and Dad decided to build an extra room over the garage. More privacy for their adult daughter, or something like that. Which means more privacy for me now.

I dump my bag on the floor just inside the door, turn on my ceiling and desk fans, and flop onto my bed. I stare at my walls for a while—plastered with paintings, sketches, and prints of my digital art—while the moving air does absolutely nothing to cool me down. Outside my door, the click of nails on the wooden stairs tells me Scrunch is on his way up. The scruffy dog jumps onto my bed and settles beside me, pinning my arm beneath his hairy body and breathing his hot stinky breath on my neck.

"Yeah, I love you too, but this isn't working." I push him away until there's enough space between the two of us.

He inches closer.

I push him again.

He settles.

I return to staring at the walls. Soon enough, my mind is flitting through ideas for a castle on a lake with a stormy sky overhead. I shouldn't start that project, though. Not until I know Mr A. T. Dawson actually wants me to do it and can pay me. I should instead begin some of the other commissioned work I scheduled for straight after finals. Not a problem, since my imagination's been buzzing with pent-up ideas for at least a month.

I cross the room and slide into my desk chair. As my giant iMac screen blinks to life, real excitement stirs somewhere in my core. Finally, *finally* I get to do what I love without the distraction of homework or tests or exams. A stupid half-smile stretches my lips as I open up my calendar,

Photoshop, and my neatly organized folder of client project details. I click the play button at the top of a recent playlist and prepare to sink into the zone.

Some time later—an hour? Two or three?—my digital canvas is covered in rough outlines and smudges of colour that will become a fantasy forest scene when I'm done. A ding from my phone pulls me out of the zone. A notification from Artser. Smiling, I minimize Photoshop and open Artster in my browser. Quicker to type on a computer keyboard than on my phone.

LuminaireX: The rainbow unicorn puke is for you. Happy no-more-exams!

I lean back in my chair, chuckling quietly as I shake my head.

AngelSH: Thanks, but you know I'm not really a rainbow girl. How about a painting of me waving some celebratory pompoms around?

LuminaireX: Right, because you're totally a pompom kinda girl.

AngelSH: Exactly.

LuminaireX: It's a good thing I've got your sarcastic sense of humour figured out by now ;)

AngelSH: You are so perceptive.

LuminaireX: Great, so I'll get right on that pompom painting! Expect a print of it in the mail.

AngelSH: Fabulous. I'll frame it and hang it on my wall.

LuminaireX: Cool, just let me know where to send it.

My smile fades the tiniest bit. I look away from the computer screen as I bite my thumbnail. Exchanging daily messages with LuminaireX—or Lex, as I've come to call him—may be one of the highlights of my life, but there's no way I'm telling him where I live. Internet relationships should stay where they belong—on the Internet. Good thing this whole conversation has been nothing more than sarcasm and silliness.

Over the sound of my music, I hear what could be the squeak of the driveway gate sliding open. I turn the volume on my computer down and cross the room to the window. Aiden's car is already down there, and Mom's car comes to a stop in front of the garage. I return to my desk and type quickly.

AngelSH: Gotta go. The pompom painting discussion will have to wait.

I hurry down the stairs with Scrunch at my side, excited that Julia's finally here. It's been far too many months since

I saw my older sister. I reach the hallway and see Mom first, laughing at something. Her smile grows wider when she notices me standing there. "My baby's finished school!" she exclaims, hurrying over and pulling me into a hug. "Well done," she adds quietly as her short hair tickles my cheek. "You've done so well."

I haven't. Aside from Art, I've barely scraped through. But I know what Mom means. You've done so well … *considering everything that's happened.* Her coddling annoys me, but I've learnt not to say anything about it.

Over Mom's shoulder, I see Julia and Josh by the front door with dad, chattering away about their mad dash through Joburg airport because they thought there was a possibility they might make their connecting flight.

"You're here!" comes a shout from the lounge. Sarah runs out and crashes into Julia and Josh, narrowly missing Dad. There's a whole lot of squealing and bouncing up and down, and suddenly I feel like the oldest person in the room because I can't remember what it's like to greet someone with so much enthusiasm. Scrunch paws at Julia's leg, madly licking her hand.

"Sophie, come join us!" Sarah calls, spotting me.

"Sophie!" Julia shouts.

Mom pushes me towards them as Aiden hurries into the room, and soon enough I'm enveloped in a group hug. Me, Sarah, Aiden, Julia, Josh. Then Mom and Dad. It's one of those rare moments in which I feel genuinely happy. Then we separate and everyone begins talking over everyone else.

"How was your last exam?"

"Did you sleep at all on the flight?"

"I feel so stinky. I *really* need a shower."

"It was okay, I guess."

"Yeah, officially on leave now."

"All my babies are back home!"

Julia and Josh start wheeling their bags towards the bedroom side of the house, still chatting with Mom and Dad. Sarah runs ahead to check if she put towels out for them. I slip away from the group and aim for the kitchen. While the rest of my family gets the squealing bounciness out of their systems, I'll get drinks ready for everyone and turn the oven on—and prepare myself to be full of smiles and happiness for the rest of the evening. Mom got up early this morning to prepare the lasagne, so all I need to do is put it—

"Oh!" I jerk backward, knocking my shoulder against the edge of the kitchen door.

The creep from the art store is standing in our kitchen.

"What—How did you—Did you *follow* me here?"

His surprised expression is quickly replaced by a grin. "Hey, it's you." He places the jug he was holding onto the nearest countertop. "As much as I'd love to say 'yes' and see how freaked out you get, I did not follow you here. This is my hotel for the next ten days."

I blink. "It is not."

"There you are," Aiden says, stepping around me and into the kitchen. "You missed the big family hug. Oh, and this is Sophie. Soph, this is Caleb. Best friend and best man."

13

"Sophie," Caleb repeats, recognition appearing in his eyes as he nods. "Sophie Henley. Younger sister of the bride and fan of craft store floors." He holds his hand out towards me as if I might possibly be interested in shaking it.

I'm not. I turn to Aiden. "You have terrible taste in best friends."

Aiden laughs. "You guys have met already?"

"Inside Marty's Arts & Crafts earlier. He was practising being a creep."

"I was practising being *friendly*," Caleb corrects. "And hoping to share the joy of true colouring in."

"You kept following me when I tried to leave. You were being a complete stalker."

"Because you made it so easy!" He laughs, then manages to stop when my glare intensifies. "I'm sorry. Really. I was pushing your buttons 'cause it was fun and I thought I'd never see you again, and you were being rude 'cause you thought you'd never see me again, so … shall we start over?"

"Wrong. I was being rude because you asked for it."

"Okay then," Aiden says loudly, slinging an arm around my shoulder and pulling me into a sideways hug. "Well, it's great that you two have already met each other, and we'll all be laughing about this one day when you're really good friends."

"I doubt it."

"And hey," he adds, "you guys have a common interest. You're both artists."

"Is that so? What do you draw, Caleb? *Random squiggles?*"

"Yes. And then I colour them in. By hand." That infuriating grin stretches across his face once more.

"No, he does what you do," Aiden says, clearly determined for us to make some kind of connection.

"Well, not exactly," Caleb says. "I don't sit on shop floors while doing my art."

"There's nothing wrong with the floor."

"Okay, I give up," Aiden says as his arm slides away from me. "I've done the introductions. You guys are on your own now. Play nicely."

He turns and leaves the kitchen. I consider following him out, but I came in here to switch the oven on, so I should at least do that. I walk around Caleb and turn the dial on the oven to the correct temperature.

"Cute tattoo," he says.

I cover my left hand, where an outline of a small star is

tattooed to the base of my thumb. I sense he's about to say something else about the star, but I'm saved from further interaction with him when Dad walks in.

"Sophie, my girl, well done on reaching the finish line." He rubs my arm and presses a brief kiss to the top of my head, and that's the end of his reaction to me having completed twelve years of schooling today. A reaction I appreciate far more than Sarah's or Mom's.

"Thanks, Dad," I murmur.

"So, Caleb," Dad says as he opens a cupboard and starts removing glasses. "What exactly is it that you do? From what Aiden's said, I gather it's something that involves a lot of travelling?"

"Oh, no, the travelling doesn't actually have anything to do with my work," Caleb says. "I just travel a lot because my work is flexible and travelling is fun. I do freelance graphic design work, mostly remote. Logos, corporate branding, website graphics, that sort of thing."

I open the oven door and move the tray to the middle level, shaking my head as I listen to Caleb and Dad. How did Aiden think that Caleb and I could possibly connect over our art when my fantasy work has absolutely nothing in common with dull, dry corporate brands? That stuff shouldn't even be classified as art. And how dare Caleb pretend he's so anti-digital art when he no doubt creates every single logo on a computer?

"And you're a teacher, right?" Caleb says to Dad.

"Yep. Physical science." Dad arranges the glasses on a tray while I remove the giant foil-covered lasagne dish from the fridge. "Which unfortunately means I'll be doing exam marking and admin until the day before the wedding."

"Ah, well, at least it's a noble profession. Oh, is this the right jug?" Caleb asks. "I was told about a glass jug, but I found several in the same cupboard. This one was the biggest."

Dad scratches his crazy science teacher hair. "To be honest, I have no idea. But I'm sure that jug will do just fine."

"That jug is fine," I mutter, opening the fridge again and looking for juice options.

"What does Mrs H. do?" Caleb enquires.

"She runs a research lab at a biotech company."

"So you bond over your mutual love of science," Caleb says with a laugh.

Dad joins in. "Yes. Anyway, it's been a busy year for her, but she's on leave from today so she can help the girls with all the last minute stuff." I close the fridge door and see him waving towards Sarah's pin board stuck to the wall beside the fridge.

"Oh, is that the magic pin board I've heard so much about?" Caleb asks.

The 'magic pin board' Aiden's always making fun of is divided into six sections for the six months leading up to the wedding. To-do notes and reminders are pinned under every month. If something wasn't done within a particular month, Sarah moved it to the next month. Since we've only got a week left to go, there isn't anywhere else to move the things that haven't yet been done. Everything has to happen within the next week.

"Hey, don't you dare knock the magic pin board," Sarah says as she hurries into the kitchen. "It's been a great help in keeping me organized with all the wedding admin."

"Yeah, you look so organized right now," I say with a smirk as she twists around, her eyes darting about the kitchen.

"Darn it, I can't remember why I—oh yes. Mom wanted me to get the savoury crackers and that biltong cream cheese dip she made this morning."

"Over there." I point to the box of crackers beside the toaster.

"Great, thanks."

Sarah gets the starter snacks together, Dad and Caleb continue to get chummy while gathering glasses and drinks, and I stare at the oven until it's hot enough to put the lasagne in. Once that's done, I paste my smile back on and join the rest of my family outside.

"You ladies are doing wedding stuff all week, right?" Aiden says as I drop into a chair beside Julia and tuck one leg beneath me.

"Well, duh," Julia says. "Remember the week before our wedding? There were a ton of things to get done."

"Cool, so we can do some touristy things then. Since, you know, we have a real tourist with us now." He gestures to Caleb.

"Are you planning to visit a game reserve?" Mom asks him.

"Yes, after the wedding," Caleb tells her. "I'm spending a

18

few days at the, uh …" He laughs. "The one I can't pronounce."

"Hluhluwe?" Sarah asks with a smile.

"That's the one."

"On your own?" Julia asks.

"Yeah, unless you guys want to join me."

"Sure, we'll see what we can organise," Julia says, looking at Josh. "We're only flying back to London after Christmas."

"You'll do a walking tour around Durban, right?" Mom says, obviously concerned that Caleb get his fill of history and culture while he's here. "And make sure you eat a bunny chow while you're at it."

Caleb leans forward, interest sparking in his eyes. "Bunny chow?"

"Wait and see, man," Aiden says. "Just wait and see."

"Oh, and the bungee swing thing," Josh adds. "At Moses Mabhida Stadium. Wasn't that on your list?"

"Oh yeah. Free falling into a stadium bowl? Sign me up."

Since everyone's busy discussing Caleb's sightseeing list, I slip my phone from my pocket and check whether Lex has replied. I know I said I had to go, but still. I'm always hoping for a message from him. Other than the message he must have sent moments after I left my room—**Cool, I'll hunt down some pompoms in the meantime**—I find no new Artster notifications. I do see that Mr A. T. Dawson has sent another email, this time asking when I can fit him into my schedule and when I'll be able to send him an invoice for the deposit I require before starting a project. He must have deemed my prices acceptable. Awesome. Every new client takes me one tiny step closer to funding my dream.

"What about you, Sophie?"

"Hmm?" I look up at the sound of my name.

"What's your favourite thing about Christmas?" Caleb asks, giving me an expectant smile. I get the feeling everyone else has already answered this and I missed it.

"Candy canes," I say, giving him the first—and briefest—answer that comes to mind. It isn't true, but this is the guy whose first words to me were an insult, and I don't feel like giving him a real answer. I turn to Julia and start asking how her photography business is going.

She gives me a look that says, *Come on, be nice.*

My responding expression of innocence says, *I have no idea what you're talking about.*

"Really?" she says in a low voice as everyone continues chatting around us. "You're gonna pretend like you weren't just totally rude to our newest guest?"

I blink. "Wait, you're assuming candy canes aren't my favourite thing about Christmas?"

She rolls her eyes. "You know I love you, but this heavy sarcasm with a side of deadpan thing you've got going on isn't the most pleasant version of you."

I give her a sweet smile. "Just like this whole mom thing you've got going on isn't the most pleasant version of you."

Her eyes widen. "Oh, you did *not* just compare me to a mom."

I poke her in the side. "I think I did."

She wraps one arm around my shoulders and tugs me

against her, making sure I'm well and truly trapped before tickling me. A yelp of laughter escapes me as I try to fight her off. "There we go," she says loudly. "Those are the squeals of delight I was looking for when I first walked back into this—Ah!" Her words are lost in laughter as I get my arms unpinned and retaliate by tickling her back.

"Really, girls?" Mom says above our noise.

We let each other go. I sit back, breathing heavily and trying not to smile. "So the photography's going well then?"

"Yeah, totally." She crosses one leg neatly over the other. "Business is booming."

Making it through the rest of the evening isn't nearly as difficult as I'd anticipated. Probably because I'm avoiding conversation with Caleb, but also because I'm happy to have Julia around again—the only member of my family I won't snap at for calling me out on my supposed 'heavy sarcasm with a side of deadpan.' I find myself getting caught up in the laughter and chatter, and there are chunks of time in which I don't even think about what happened last Christmas.

We end the evening slumped sleepily in the chairs outside, mosquitoes and other bugs buzzing around the lights, and the evening breeze doing its best to provide us with some relief from the heat. Not that it helps much when I'm sandwiched in between Julia and Sarah on the same couch. I think our arms are sticking together.

Mom places a bowl of chocolate covered nuts on the table, pushes Scrunch off her chair, and sits with a sigh. "I'm sure there was a slab of chocolate too, but I can't find it."

"The monkeys probably stole it," Sarah says.

Caleb, Jules and Josh start laughing, but Sarah says, "I'm not joking. Monkeys come in through the kitchen windows all the time. It's a real problem."

"I told you we need to move the fruit away from the window and cover it," Dad says to Mom.

"That doesn't stop them," Mom tells him. "If the windows are open, they'll climb inside, kick stuff off the counter, and take whatever food they can find."

"Damn monkeys," I mutter, remembering the time they helped themselves to the piece of cake I brought home from the cafe next to the craft store.

"Sophie," Mom scolds as my language triggers her swear word detector.

"Sorry."

"Okay, well as much as I want to stay up for the rest of the night," Mom says around a yawn, "I can't keep my eyes open. You kids can lock up when you go to bed."

"Agreed," Dad says. "Night, everyone." He stands and follows her into the house.

Caleb chuckles and reaches for the bowl on the table. "I love being twenty-five and getting called a kid."

"We'll probably always be 'kids' to our parents," Aiden says, "no matter how grown-up we feel."

Caleb throws a chocolate covered nut at Aiden. "I never said I feel grown-up."

Aiden scrambles to catch the nut, but misses. "Dude, you play around with shapes on a computer for a living. You'll probably never grow up."

"You're just jealous," Caleb says, managing to simultaneously speak, grin, and crunch on a handful of nuts.

"I am," Aiden says with a sigh. "The university is sucking the life out of my soul these days."

"Come travel the world with me. You can bring Sarah with if she promises not to behave."

"So generous of you," Sarah says.

Julia, who's been flicking through photos on her phone and showing them to me—urban scenes, English countryside, the occasional wedding—laughs and sticks another one under my nose. "Look at this cat. Fattest thing I've ever seen, but it was *determined* to get up that wall because there was a bird sitting on top of it."

I chuckle at the black and white photo where Julia's caught the moment in which the world's roundest cat is reaching upward across a graffiti covered brick wall for a bird that was no doubt mocking the cat for its efforts.

Julia scrolls quickly through more photos, this time of people gathered in a pub. Scenes washed in orange-brown tones and warm light. "What's Lacey doing while you're here?" she asks, directing her question towards Caleb.

"Lacey? You know Lacey and I broke up like four months ago, right?"

"Oh." Julia pauses in her picture-scrolling and lowers her

phone. "Who was the girl you were in Australia with?"

"Janine.

"Ah. I thought you were with Janine before Lacey."

"That was Jenny," Caleb says. "I can understand your confusion."

"So who's waiting for you back home?" Julia asks.

"Currently? Nobody."

Quite the serial dater, I think to myself, but fortunately I'm too sleepy to say the words out loud.

"Hey, remember this one," Julia says to me, distracted already by another photo. "It must be from, like, ten Christmases ago."

The photo shows Sarah, Julia and I clinging to Dad's body while trying to reach a large gift box he's holding over his head.

"Hmm. It's not unlike the cat photo," I say after examining it.

Julia dissolves into giggles. "I hadn't thought of that." She passes her phone around so everyone can take a look.

"Oh, you used to be blonde, Sophie," Caleb says, examining the photo.

"Mm hmm." I push my fingers through my dark hair. I redid the roots last week when I was supposed to be studying *Othello* for my English Lit final.

"Like an angel," Julia says, leaning her head on my shoulder.

I groan. "Remember how they always used to make me play the angel for nativity plays at pre-school? All the girls wanted to be Mary, but I was always stuck as an angel."

"A beautiful angel," Julia murmurs sleepily.

"So you didn't like being blonde?" Caleb asks.

"What do you think?" I mean, duh. Obviously not. That's why I changed the colour.

"Soph," Julia murmurs. "You don't have to be so hostile."

I close my eyes and rest my head against hers. "It's my default setting."

"It wasn't always."

I don't bother answering her, and she's so sleepy she probably doesn't notice.

My eyes slide closed. Soft chatter continues around me, lulling me towards sleep.

"I'm going to bed," Sarah announces, startling me awake as she pushes herself up from the couch. "I have to pick up my dress in the morning, and then … I don't know. A hundred other things I can't remember right now."

"I'm sure it's all on the magic pin board," Aiden says, followed by "Ow!" when Sarah punches his arm.

"Stop making fun of my organizational system, otherwise I'll make you do everything left on the list."

"I love the magic pin board," Aiden says quickly. "The magic pin board is amazing."

"It is," Sarah says.

"Um, yeah, it is late," I say as I stifle a yawn. Especially considering my day began at three this morning when I got up to do my final cramming for Art History.

I help the others carry all the cushions inside—in case it rains during the night—which means we're all breaking out

25

in a sweat by the time we're done and I'm locking the door. I wipe my hand across my brow as I wait for everyone to trail out of the lounge so I can turn the lights off and the house alarm on. Hopefully no one hogs the bathroom for too long. I don't care how late it is, I'm not getting into bed without drenching myself in cold water first.

Up in the attic, I dig around in my pyjama drawer until I find a lightweight dressing gown. It's too hot to comfortably add *any* additional layer over my pyjamas, but with extra guys now occupying the house, I'm not about to be caught in just a pair of boxers and a tank top. The moment the bathroom's free, I take my chance. I force myself to stand beneath the shockingly cold stream of water without turning on the hot tap, knowing I'll be grateful for it the moment I step out of the shower. After dressing quickly, I exit the bathroom and find—the only person I'm not interested in talking to. Obviously.

Caleb gives me a smile.

I sigh and head past him.

"You know, this usually works for people." I turn at the foot of the stairs and look back to find him gesturing to his face.

"What, your irresistible charm?" He can't be referring to his good looks. Nobody's actually that arrogant, are they?

"No, the smile." His grin stretches even wider. "Doesn't it make you want to smile back?"

My expression remains impassive. "Nope."

"Interesting. Most people, when greeted with a smile, respond by smiling back."

I respond by raising an eyebrow.

He sighs. "I find this mildly discouraging—

"Good."

"—but I will not be deterred."

"Ugh. Please be deterred."

"I'll get a smile out of you yet, Sophie Henley."

"Wonderful," I reply, my deadpan expression still firmly in place as I turn and climb the stairs.

Back in my room, I grab my phone and check for messages while climbing into bed. Nothing from Lex. I try to pretend it doesn't leave me feeling disappointed.

AngelSH: Hey. I'm a new follower of yours and just wanted to say how amazing your art is. I also really appreciate the tutorials you post on your website sometimes. I've already learned a whole lot from them, so I just thought I should take a moment to thank you personally :-)

LuminaireX: Hey, thanks very much. You're welcome :-)

AngelSH: You probably get a billion messages like this all the time, but if you have a free moment, do you mind if I ask you a question or two?

LuminaireX: Sure, fire away.

AngelSH: Thank you!

AngelSH: P.S. 'A question or two' actually means, like, fifty. So feel free to ignore me when you run out of time ;-)

LuminaireX: LOL, not a prob :)

3

I SLEEP LATER THAN I'VE SLEPT IN AGES. WELL, THE SLEEP part doesn't last long after the sun brightens my room, but I lie in bed with half-closed eyelids, listening to the faint noises from downstairs and glorying in the fact that Mom isn't about to bang on my door and yell, "Are you studying yet?" As far as I know, I don't have to do anything wedding related until tonight, so I can stay in bed all day if I want to.

When my phone buzzes briefly against my bedside table, I turn over and reach for it, hoping it's Lex. Instead, I see a message from Isabelle containing an image of a baby owl with big sad eyes. The text overlay on the picture reads, 'Don't want to be owl by myself.' I've barely had time to roll my eyes when a second message appears.

Isabelle: I know you've finished exams, so you have no excuse to keep avoiding me. I'm coming over.

I let out a sleepy moan. I don't feel like social interaction with my once-best-friend right now. Or ever, perhaps. Why can't I just grab a bowl of cereal and a sketchpad and hide in my room for the whole day? Or in the garage with my easel. Today feels like the perfect day for real paints and brushes.

Before I can think of how to keep Isabelle out of my house, another message pops up.

Isabelle: And don't tell me you're not home. I just saw your mom at PnP.

Ugh. Thanks a lot, Mom. I pull a pillow over my head and blot out the world. Perhaps if I pretend to be fast asleep, Isabelle won't stay.

No such luck. Minutes later, my door opens and a bright voice says, "Morning, Sophie!" Then Scrunch barks and lands on top of me, and my involuntary groan gives me away. "We're finished school!" Isabelle sings. Scrunch jumps off the bed, and the mattress moves as Isabelle sits.

I turn over slowly and push myself up. "Um, hi."

"Did you get my messages?" She tucks her messy blonde hair behind one ear and hands me a takeaway plastic cup containing a green drink.

"Sort of. I was too sleepy to reply." *Liar, liar, Sophie Henley.* I eye the green drink with suspicion. "What's this?"

"Apple, kale, cucumber and … I don't know. Some other green stuff."

"You're making me drink salad for breakfast?"

30

"It's nice," she insists. "Just try it."

I take a tentative sip and find that it doesn't taste as bad as I expected. I wouldn't go as far as calling it 'nice,' but it's drinkable.

"So," she says. "I counted the weeks. You managed to go almost two months this time."

"Two months?"

"Avoiding your one and only friend. Impressive, considering we live in the same road."

"I haven't been avoiding you," I say, trying to make it sound like the truth. "I had finals, remember? And now there are a million annoyingly happy people in my house. I was trying to save you from all the craziness. And you're not my only friend, by the way."

"Your internet bestie doesn't count."

"He does."

"Great, so you have two friends. You've never met the one, and you try your best never to see the other. That isn't healthy, Soph."

I place the juice on my bedside table before squirming back beneath the covers. "I don't have to listen to this on my first official day of freedom," I mumble.

Isabelle tugs the duvet back and whacks me over the head with a cushion. "Yes you do."

"Hey!" I cover my head with my hands.

"Stop being such a mopey loner!" The cushion smacks my head a second time.

I push her away and sit up. Once I've forced my tangled hair out of the way, I give her a grumpy look. "You know why I'm a mopey loner."

"No." She leans back on her elbows. "I don't."

"You're kidding, right?"

"No, I'm not kidding. I am never, *ever* going to do what Braden did, so you have zero reason to keep distancing yourself from me."

I tilt my head back against the wall and shut my eyes. My right thumb rubs the skin at the base of my left thumb. The position of my star tattoo.

"Seriously, Soph. We've been friends since pre-school. Haven't you figured out by now that I'm not going anywhere?"

I wait a while before speaking. Eventually I open my eyes and stare past Isabelle at the wall on the other side of my room. "I'm sorry. I do know that. It's just … life's easier when I don't have to care about other people."

"Lazy bum." Isabelle pokes me with her toe. "Life isn't supposed to be easy. Besides, that's total nonsense. Life is definitely easier when you have friends to rely on."

Right. Unless they're the kind of friends who disappear when the going gets tough. But Isabelle was never in that category, so I should stop freaking out and trying to hide every time she wants to hang out and be … well, friends. I reach for the plastic cup. "Thanks for the juice. Do you want some?"

"Nah, I drank mine on the way here." She lets out a long breath, leans back, and crosses one leg over the other. "So now what?"

"Now what what?"

"Now that school's finished, what are you doing next aside from sleeping in?"

I lean back against the pillows. "You know what I'm doing next."

"You're going to follow your 'never fall in love again' rule, hide from everyone for the rest of your life, and become a reclusive artist."

"Basically, yes. With some exotic travels thrown in, which I can totally do on my own. And you—" I point at her "—are going to study boring theology."

"I think you mean fascinating. And didn't we just talk about how you being reclusive isn't healthy?"

"No, we spoke about how I have two amazing friends and it doesn't matter that I've never met one of them in real life."

Isabelle purses her lips. "I think university would be good for you."

I groan and knock my head against the wall—harder than I'd intended—and almost spill green juice down the front of my pyjamas. "What would be the point in me going to university? I already know how to do what I want to do. I've *been* doing it for years."

"I'm sure there's more you could learn."

"I'm sure there is, but I don't have to learn it at a university."

"A course of some sort?"

"Isabelle, no," I say firmly. "I've decided what course my life will take next, and you're not going to change my mind."

"Fine." Her gaze moves around my room, taking in

whatever new paintings I've added to the walls since she was last in here. "Hey, is that your sister's book?" she asks, nodding towards my bedside table where Sarah's book is at the bottom of a pile of school textbooks—which I need to hide, throw away, or burn some time soon.

"Yes, that's her first one. Second one will be out soon, I think."

"Oh my gosh, can I see it?" She sits up quickly. I reach over, push the textbooks to the edge of the table, and pass the novel to Isabelle. "And it's *signed*!" she exclaims, paging carefully through it as if it's breakable. "This is so awesome. You're related to someone famous, Sophie!"

"I guess. Sort of."

Isabelle looks up. "You are. Didn't this book do really well when it came out?"

"Um, I think so. It was on a list or something."

"What list?"

"I don't know what list. I don't know about book stuff."

"You are a terrible sister, Sophie Henley," Isabelle jokes. "And can I please borrow this?"

"Sure." I try to smile, but it's difficult when I'm thinking of just how terrible a sister I really am. I haven't even read Sarah's book. It's her dream come true, but I've been too distracted by art and schoolwork and Braden-related pain to get past the title page she autographed.

My phone shudders against my bedside table. I pick it up, welcoming the interruption to my thoughts.

"Ooh, is that your other *friend*?" Isabelle asks, managing to sound as mature as a six-year-old.

"No." I try to keep the disappointment from my voice as I open the notification. "Just someone liking my stuff on Artster."

"Do you know his name yet?"

"Who, Lex?"

"Yes. You said that isn't actually his name, right? So what's his real name?"

I lock my phone and toss it onto the bed beside me. "It doesn't matter. I call him Lex, and he's fine with that."

"Have you seen a picture of him?" she asks, twisting a strand of hair around her finger.

"Come on, you aren't really that shallow, are you?"

"What, I'm just curious. Aren't you?"

"Not really." The look she points my way tells me she doesn't believe me for a second. "Seriously, it doesn't matter to me. In my head he's a skinny Asian guy called Lex, and I'm happy with that."

She lets out a guffaw of laughter. "A skinny Asian guy? Where'd you get that idea from?"

"From his Artster profile picture. It's a painting he did of an anime character a while back. Didn't I show you?"

"No. I think we've already established that you've been mastering the art of avoidance for the past year." She sits up as I unlock my phone and open Artster. "LuminaireX," she says, her voice low and mysterious. "Why X? What could that possibly mean?"

"Uh, that Luminaire was already taken?"

"Oh. Probably."

I tap Lex's profile picture to enlarge it before holding the

35

phone up. "See? Anime character."

"Hmm. Interesting. I assume he looks nothing like this in real life, though."

"So what? That's how I picture him." I turn the phone back around to face me and zoom in on the digital painting.

"What if he's really old?" Isabelle says. "That would be creepy."

"I don't think he's old. He doesn't talk like an old person."

"Maybe he's ugly."

"Why do you assume he's ugly just because he doesn't use an actual photo of himself? And what does it matter if he's ugly? I don't talk to him every day because he might be hot. I talk to him every day because I enjoy it."

Isabelle pauses before saying, "You talk to him every day?"

"Well … yes. You know. Just a few messages."

Her lips spread into a slow smile, and I know exactly where she's going next. "Oh my goodness. You're totally in love with this guy."

"No."

"Yes you are. You're already breaking your own rule."

"I'm in love with his *art*, Iz. There's a difference." I run my eyes over the expertly painted spiky hair and the signature in the bottom right corner. A loop-scribble-loop I know as well as my own signature.

Isabelle laughs and says in a sing-song voice, "So-phie's in lo-ove."

"Shut up." I lean over and smack my phone down on the

bedside table. "I'm not in love with anyone."

But the terrifying truth is that I am. Because Lex is the one exception I've allowed myself. The one guy it's okay to fall for, because I know I'll never meet him in real life. I'll never have him. And if I never have him, I can never lose him.

At least, that's what I keep telling myself.

"Sophie!"

The shout comes from the direction of the stairs, accompanied by hurried footsteps. A moment later, Sarah appears in my doorway looking flustered. "Soph, I need help."

LuminaireX: Awesome job with the hair on Mystique. It came out so well.

AngelSH: Thanks! I tried that other video tutorial you suggested, and it was such a help. Thank you.

LuminaireX: You welcome.

AngelSH: You're

AngelSH: OMG I'm so sorry.

AngelSH: I can't believe I just did that.

AngelSH: My sister's an English pro and she's forever correcting the things I say and write. It's super annoying, and then I realised recently that I've started doing it too!!! *slinking away in embarrassment now*

LuminaireX: LOL, don't worry about it. YOU'RE right after all ;-) I'll try not to be a lazy typist.

AngelSH: I'm so sorry. You can type however you want.

LuminaireX: I'm on a computer right now. I have no excuse for lazy typing.

AngelSH: Okay. Anyway, thanks again, LX.

LuminaireX: Sure thing, ASH ;)

AngelSH: Hey Lex, how'd you do the wings on those mini dragon-like creatures in the background on your latest piece?

AngelSH: Sorry. Autocorrect. LX.

LuminaireX: No prob. I kinda like Lex. Can I call you Ash?

AngelSH: You already call me ASH.

LuminaireX: True. But in my head it sounds like A-S-H. Ash is easier.

AngelSH: LOL. Same. My brain says L-X, but Lex is easier.

LuminaireX: Hi, Ash, I'm Lex. Nice to meet you :-)

AngelSH: Hi :-) So ... the wings?

LuminaireX: Right. I cheated. It was actually a brush. I'll find the link for you.

AngelSH: Thanks so much.

LuminaireX: But then you have to show me the finished piece.

AngelSH: Sure. I'll put it in my Artster gallery.

LuminaireX: You doing something fairy-ish?

AngelSH: No.

LuminaireX: Dragon-ish?

AngelSH: No.

LuminaireX: Angel-ish?

AngelSH: No.

LuminaireX: For someone with the word 'angel' in their username, you don't do nearly nearly enough angel art.

AngelSH: LOL, that's not why I have the word 'angel' in my username.

LuminaireX: Ooh, do tell.

AngelSH: Nope, sorry, not telling you that one ;-)

LuminaireX: Well at least tell me what you're planning to do with the wings brush.

AngelSH: You'll think it's strange. I'd rather you wait and see the finished product.

LuminaireX: Promise I won't think it's strange. (Or if I do, I won't tell you :P)

AngelSH: Okay …

AngelSH: Fine …

AngelSH: I'm doing a close-up of a face and I thought those wings would look cool as eyelashes. I could draw them from scratch, but a brush is quicker (even if it is cheating ;-))

LuminaireX: Hmm. Eyelashes. That could actually work.

AngelSH: Thanks :)

4

"What do you need help with?" I ask Sarah. "Did something go wrong?"

"It's just … ugh, everything's happening at once and I can't do it all," she moans, leaning against the door frame. "I have to pick up my dress in twenty minutes, and there were adjustments last time, so we need to check that everything fits properly, but now Mrs Govender says the favours are ready for collection, and she's leaving for the airport in an hour. The airport! Like, to go overseas! Which she definitely failed to mention to me up until ten minutes ago. And Mom and Dad are shopping, and Jules and Josh went for a run and haven't come back yet, and Aiden's at the printers getting the menus done, and Mrs Govender's like, 'Hello, my sweetie. You need to come and pick these up now or you won't get them until after Christmas.' Christmas! She *knows* I'm getting married in a week and that I'm stressed

41

about everything, so why would she make a joke like that? And her house is in the opposite direction to where the dressmaker is, and I can't reschedule with the dressmaker because she's totally booked up right now and, to be honest, she kinda scares me. And—"

"Calm down, Sarah." I push the duvet away and climb out of the bed. "This isn't a big deal." Okay, perhaps not the best choice of words. *Everything* is a big deal to Sarah right now. "I'll take Mom's car and go pick up the favours. Just don't tell her. Isabelle can come with me. You've also got a learner's, right, Iz?" I turn back to look at her, and she nods.

"Sophie, two learner's licences—"

"—don't equal a full licence," I say to Sarah. "I know. But no one's going to stop us. It'll be fine. I'll be showered in five minutes, then Iz and I can go."

"I …" Sarah looks between the two of us, her desperation to get these silly wedding favours conflicting with her law-abiding nature. "Maybe if I drive really quickly, I can do both. I'll be a bit late for the dressmaker, but that should—"

"I can go with Sophie," a voice shouts from the bottom of the stairs.

I frown at Sarah. "Is that Caleb?" Though I know he can't see me standing here in my skimpy PJs, I automatically take a step back.

"I have a licence," he calls up to us.

Sarah turns and looks down the stairs. "I'm not sure your licence counts here."

"And eavesdropping is rude," I add loudly.

"My licence does count," he says. "At least, it does according to a page about foreign travel advice on the UK government website."

"People actually look at sites like that?" I mutter to Sarah.

Instead of answering me, she shouts back down the stairs, "Thank you! You're a lifesaver, Caleb."

"I can drive, if you want," Caleb says ten minutes later as we hurry into the garage.

"I know how to drive," I tell him, making my way around the side of Mom's car. The three of us climb in— Isabelle taking the back seat—and I slam my door closed a little too hard. Starting the ignition, it occurs to me that perhaps I should have let Caleb drive. If I stall the car or roll backwards on a hill, it'll be totally humiliating after my 'I know how to drive.' But I can't bring myself to hand over the keys.

I successfully reverse down the driveway and out of the gate, which gives me enough confidence to relax just a bit. *I can do this. I will not make a fool of myself.*

"Well done," Caleb says as I pull off smoothly and head up the road.

"Shut up," I mumble.

"Oh, can you drop me off at home, Soph?" Isabelle asks, poking her head forward between my seat and Caleb's.

43

"Mom wants me to help with lunch. The grandparents are visiting."

Terrific. I won't even have Isabelle as a buffer.

In the twenty seconds or so that it takes me to drive to Isabelle's house, she questions Caleb, and he gives her the shortened version of everything I heard last night. "Bye, Soph," she says as she jumps out. "Don't be a stranger."

"Of course not," I say in a cheerful tone, as if me being a stranger is unheard of. "Um, tell your parents I say hi," I add. I think that's the kind of thing I used to say before I became socially messed up. Isabelle will appreciate it.

"Sure," she calls back, waving at me as she walks through her gate.

I pull away from Isabelle's house, waiting for Caleb to say something. It doesn't take long. As we reach the end of the street, he shifts around, apparently making himself more comfortable, and says, "Tell me about your art."

Right. Like I'm really going to admit that I digitally paint dragons, fairies, angels, demons and dozens of other fantasy elements to the guy who designs corporate logos. "Um … it's art. Some of it's digital. Some of it isn't. Sometimes I'm in my room on an iMac. Sometimes I'm in the garage with an easel and paints."

"iMac, awesome. Those are amazing."

For some reason I feel the need to justify why I have a super expensive computer. As if I should explain to him that I started saving after selling my very first digital art several years ago—back when I used the school art department's computers and software—until I could afford the tools I really wanted. But, I remind myself, I don't have to explain a single thing to Caleb. So I simply go with, "Yeah."

"And it's great that you use the real thing too," he says. "Nothing quite like the feel of real paint moving across a canvas at the tip of a real paintbrush."

Again, I go with the one-word answer: "Yeah."

"I've played around with just about everything," he says.

"Including colouring in?" Oops, that one slipped out.

Despite my sarcasm, Caleb's response is as good-natured as ever. "Will you ever let that one go?"

I shrug and look away from the road for a second to turn up the volume on the radio. Then I point my eyes forward once more and try to relax my rigid frame. I'm not entirely comfortable yet with driving, but there's no need for Caleb to know that. From the corner of my eye, I see his hand reaching for the volume button. The music quietens. "So what are these wedding favours we're picking up?" he asks.

I consider turning the music up again, but he'll most likely turn it down. Again and again. And then we'll have an accident because I'm too busy fighting over the stupid radio volume. "Jars of jam," I tell him.

He laughs—which I'm quickly learning is his response to most things—but when I don't join in, he stops. "I can't tell if you're being serious."

"I am."

"Oh. Okay." He shifts around in his seat a bit more. "So … jam, huh."

I guess I'm not going to get away with zero conversation.

"Mrs Govender makes jam. It's her thing. She's a good family friend of ours, so we've been on the receiving end of a lot of jam over the years. Sarah loves it, so she thought it would be cute to put jam in little jars with a thank-you label on each one for each wedding guest. Mrs Govender was thrilled to be involved in some way."

"Okay, that's less weird than it initially sounded."

"Exactly."

"It's actually pretty cool."

"It is."

"You're not very good at this."

Fortunately, the traffic light up ahead turns red, giving me a chance to step on the brake and take a moment to fix Caleb with my favourite deadpan expression. "Are you referring to my conversation skills?"

"What conversation skills? Okay, I'm kidding!" he adds hastily as my eyes widen. "It's just that you're not giving me much to work with."

"Could that possibly be because I'm concentrating on driving?"

"It could, I guess. But most likely your responses would be just as short if you weren't behind the wheel of a car. Come on, interact." He pokes my arm. "Don't be so lifeless."

"Don't poke the driver."

I jump as the car behind me hoots. My eyes flash to the traffic light and find it green. Panicking, I put the car in gear and step on the accelerator a little too hard. The car lurches forward and Caleb says, "Whoa! Not so lifeless after all, I see."

"Stop distracting me."

"You sure you don't want me to drive?"

"Shut up."

He doesn't listen, of course, but he moves from direct questions to random passing comments, which means I don't have to respond.

When we reach Mrs Govender's house, I successfully park the car without bumping into the curb. I climb out, walk to her gate, and press the buzzer. It doesn't make a noise, which I'm not sure is normal. Hopefully Mrs Govender heard something inside the house. Caleb, looking exceedingly laid back with his hands in the pockets of his shorts, joins me at the gate. He looks around, taking in the neighbourhood while I press the button a second time.

Birds twitter nearby, the morning sun bakes my head, and nobody opens the gate.

"Crap," I murmur, standing on tiptoe and trying to see over the gate, which has wooden slats between the metal bars so that people can't look through it. I can just see onto the porch, where the front door is closed, as are the curtains.

"There are way too many walls and fences and gates around here," Caleb observes. "Not exactly welcoming, is it?"

"Yeah, well, we don't want to welcome criminals onto our properties." I retrieve my phone from the car and search for Mrs Govender's number, despite the fact that I'm fairly certain I don't have it. Once I've confirmed that her number is nowhere on my phone, I call Sarah. Twice. And she doesn't answer either time, because her intimidating dressmaker's probably told her to put her phone on silent during fittings.

"Want me to lift you up so you can climb over the wall?" Caleb asks.

"No. Please don't touch me."

He laughs. "That's the part that bothers you? More than the criminal activity?"

I open my mouth to tell him he's not being helpful, but that's the moment I hear a door opening. I rise onto my toes again and see Mrs Govender, slightly bent and moving as slowly as she always does, wheeling a suitcase through her open front door and onto the porch. "Mrs Govender," I call, raising my arm and waving it. "It's Sophie. I'm here for the miniature jam jars."

"Oh, yes, of course." She waves back to me before heading into the house. Moments later, the gate slides open. Caleb and I walk up to the porch. "Sorry, my dear," she says as she returns. "Were you out there for long?"

"Um, not too long. I rang the gate buzzer a few times, but—"

"Oh, it's not working." She gives me an apologetic smile. "So sorry, dear. Come inside. The jams are here in the entrance hall." We step inside and find four shallow cardboard boxes piled on top of each other. Rows of little jam jars are visible in the top box. I pick up the top two boxes, and Caleb lifts the bottom two.

"Thank you so much, Mrs Govender," I say as we walk back out to the porch. "Sarah's so grateful to you for doing this. She's sorry she couldn't pick up the favours herself."

"Oh, of course, of course. Brides get busy, I know."

"Where are you off to?" Caleb asks, nodding to the suitcase.

"India," she tells him, appearing delighted that he asked. "To visit my family for Christmas."

"Oh, fantastic. What a marvellous adventure."

"Two out of five grandchildren have arrived since I last visited," she says to him, leaning in as if sharing a secret, "so it will be my first time seeing them."

"Ah, that's amazing. Have a wonderful time, Mrs Govender," he adds as we step down onto the driveway. I want to roll my eyes. Does he always have to be so annoyingly friendly?

He sits in the passenger seat with all four boxes piled on top of him. Mindful of the glass jars, I try to take off as smoothly as I can. Instead, the car moves jerkily forward before settling into smooth motion. Thankfully, Caleb has the decency to wait at least a minute before politely asking, "So when are you doing your driver's test?"

"In January. I turned eighteen during finals, so I didn't have time to do it then."

"Okay. Well, you've got time to practise a little more before then."

I press my lips together and ignore his thinly veiled insult.

He remains quiet until I turn back into my road. "So why

were you at the craft store for so long yesterday? I know you said there's nothing wrong with the floor, but surely it's more comfortable to tap your iPad at home?"

I ignore the 'tap your iPad' part and say, "I was waiting for Sarah to pick me up after work."

"Okay. Too far to walk?"

I can't tell if it's a genuine question, or if he's trying to hint that I'm too lazy to walk the few kilometres home. "No, it isn't too far, but it isn't safe either."

"Even during the day?"

"Well, I'm sure it's safer during the day than at night, but I'd rather not risk it. I don't want to end up mugged, raped and buried alive in the cemetery across the road." I nod my head to the side, gesturing towards the fence and the headstones beyond.

"Has that actually happened?"

"Not often, but yes. Well, I'm not sure if the burying alive part has happened, but someone definitely tried that at least once. And the other stuff … yeah. That happens." I slow down as I approach home.

"Hey, look at that," Caleb says. "We made it home alive."

I refrain from commenting as I stop at the bottom of the driveway, pull the handbrake up, and push the button to open the gate. I rev the engine and release the handbrake— and that's when I stall.

"Brilliant," I mutter.

Beside me, Caleb laughs.

Obviously.

After parking Mom's car, we carry the boxes of jam inside. Julia and Josh have returned from their morning run and are stretching in the kitchen, and Mom and Dad are unpacking groceries from shopping bags. Caleb and I stack the jam boxes on top of each other on one side of the counter while Caleb asks Josh if he's recovered from his over-exertion yet.

"Gimme a hug," Julia says to me, opening her sweaty arms.

"Ew, no." I side-step out of the way before she can catch me.

As I leave the kitchen, Mom follows me out and pulls me aside. "Honey, are you … okay?"

Well that came out of nowhere. "Yes. Why wouldn't I be okay?"

"You look kind of … down."

"Well I'm not down, I'm normal."

"I don't want you to be normal, Soph, I want you to be *more than that*," Mom says, peering at me with such earnest that it's as if she hopes her expression alone could somehow lift my mood. "This is such an exciting time for everyone. I want you to be as happy as the rest of us."

"I am happy." I realise a moment later that my blank expression might not convey this, so I give Mom a smile. "See?"

She doesn't seem convinced. "Sophie," she says slowly, "if you were depressed, you'd tell me, right?"

"I'm not depressed, Mom."

"Are you sure?"

51

"Yes. My baseline happiness level just sits a bit lower now than it once did."

"But that's not good. Maybe that means that you're—"

"It doesn't. It means I'm fine, I promise." I give Mom a reassuring pat on the arm before turning and heading for my room. I'm pretty sure I'm right. If I was on the brink of depression, I'd know. I'd feel myself falling, and nothing—not my drawing or Lex or seeing Julia for the first time in months—would be able to catch me.

I'm not depressed. I'm different now, that's all.

LuminaireX: Wow, darkness alert. What's up with your gallery lately? I mean, it's awesome stuff, but ... pretty dark.

AngelSH: Sorry. Just had a few bad days, that's all. Sometimes the darkness needs to crawl out onto paper. Better to get it out than to keep it locked inside, you know?

LuminaireX: Sure.

LuminaireX: I get that.

LuminaireX: I mean, if I were to draw the darkness crawling out of me, it would probably be an ant ...

AngelSH: Oh come on. Don't all artists have tortured souls?

LuminaireX: Sure. My ant is tied up. Tortured. Screaming ...

AngelSH: I can't take my darkness seriously when you're around.

LuminaireX: My work here is done.

AngelSH: :P

AngelSH: Seriously, though. Don't you have anything in your life that causes you to have dark moments?

LuminaireX: Uh ... my parents, I guess.

AngelSH: Are they divorced?

LuminaireX: Yeah. A while back. I was 11.

AngelSH: Sorry :-(

LuminaireX: It wouldn't be too bad if they could just get along, but years later they still can't have a civil conversation. Always end up shouting at each other.

AngelSH: That really sucks. What do you do when that happens?

LuminaireX: Opposite of what you do. Bright, colourful, happy paintings ;-)

AngelSH: LOL, that's probably a better idea.

LuminaireX: Hey, whatever works for you :)

"LIVI!" SARAH SQUEALS AND RUNS INTO THE ARMS OF HER
best friend as we enter the school hall. I hang back in the
doorway, wondering if there's any way I can still get out of
this dance lesson.

"One week, Sarah," Livi says, gripping Sarah's arms
tightly. "One week and then you're freaking *getting married!*"

"I know!"

This is followed by more squealing—Julia joins in this
time—which almost sends me marching back out to the
parking lot. Seriously, how much squealing can possibly be
involved in one wedding? Surely we've reached our squeal
quota by now?

"Where's Adam?" Sarah asks, referring to her other good
friend and Livi's boyfriend. "I thought he was going to
come along and laugh at us."

"Yeah, but then he thought he'd feel a bit spare just

hanging around, since he isn't part of the bridal party."

"Oh, but I haven't seen him yet since you guys arrived. I wanted to—"

"Is everybody here?" The shrill voice comes from a corner of the hall where a woman and a young boy are leaning over a laptop and speakers set up on a table. The woman pushes away from the table and comes towards us in high-heeled dance shoes. Her eyebrows are penciled on just a little too high, and her blue-black hair is in need of a touch-up where her grey roots are showing through. "Sarah, is this everyone?" she asks in an accent that sounds … French?

"Um, yes, I think so." Sarah looks at us.

"Yeah, this is everyone from the bridal party," Aiden says. "Three bridesmaids—Jules, Sophie and Livi—and three groomsmen—Caleb, Josh and Nick."

"Wonderful, wonderful," the dance instructor says. "I am Lucille, and I will be teaching you a simple dance so you do not look ridiculous at the wedding." She extends an arm elegantly towards the bridal couple. "Sarah and Aiden, since you have been here before, why don't you give us a demonstration of what you remember?"

"Oh. Uh, okay." Sarah turns to Aiden with wide eyes as Lucille nods to the boy standing by the table.

"It's fine, we've been practising," Aiden says in a low voice.

"I know, but I thought we'd all be doing this lesson *together*, without people watching us."

"I think you need to get used to people watching you,

Sezzie," Livi says loudly. "It's what everyone's going to be doing next Saturday."

Tinny music echoes across the hall as Sarah and Aiden hurry to get into position. Lucille counts them in, and they begin dancing. Their movements are a little stiff, and they stumble here and there, but they keep mostly in time to the music. When Aiden twirls Sarah around and ends off by dipping her down, both Livi and Julia let out an audible sigh.

I resist the urge to mime throwing up, but clearly I don't hide my distaste well enough, because Caleb asks innocently, "Something wrong?"

I take a purposeful step away from him. Even if I felt like talking to him, how would I explain what's wrong. Dancing just … isn't for me anymore. I think I might have enjoyed it once upon a time—I have vague memories of jumping around in my pyjamas with Isabelle in front of the radio in her bedroom—but that feels like a lifetime ago. A lifetime before Braden. Now it just seems too … silly-happy.

The music stops. "That was good," Lucille says, clapping for Sarah and Aiden. "Now everyone else pair up and we will begin the lesson. Aiden, you will help me demonstrate."

"Oh, uh, sure."

Julia and Josh will obviously dance together, so I head straight for Nick. As Aiden's closest friend here in South Africa, Nick isn't a stranger to me. Dancing with him will be fine. Civilized. A little awkward, but not nearly as unpleasant as dancing with Caleb. "I apologise in advance," Nick says as I step up to him, "because I'm pretty sure I'm going to stand on your feet at some point."

Behind me, Livi introduces herself to Caleb.

"No, no, no," Lucille says. "Mismatched heights. You go with you—" she pulls me away from Nick and pushes Livi into my place "—and you go with you." She twists me around and steers me towards Caleb.

Brilliant. Somewhere out there, the universe is laughing at me.

"So, not only do I have to endure this stupid dancing thing," I mutter, "I have to do it with the guy who doesn't know how to mind his own business."

"Hey, I take offense to that," Caleb says. "This 'dancing thing' is not stupid."

"You're kidding, right? This is the biggest waste of time ever. Do you really think we're all going to look good out there on a dance floor after only one or two lessons? No, this is all super awkward. We'd be better off swaying aimlessly to the—"

A tight grip latches onto my arm and drags me towards the hall door. I stumble after Sarah as she pulls me into the hallway outside. "Jeez, Sarah, what are you—"

"Listen up," she says fiercely. "I have been patient with you for months. I've given you space, I've comforted you, I've put up with your mood swings, I've excused your rudeness. I've done *everything* I could to be supportive after what happened with Braden. But I'm done. This is *my* time now. This is the only wedding I get, and I will not have you making it unpleasant for everyone else. You will be friendly, you will keep your never-ending rude comments to yourself, and you will pretend you're having a good time no matter how much you want to throw up all over my happiness. Okay?" I'm so shocked by Sarah's uncharacteristic outburst that I can't think of a single thing to say. "Good," she says. She swings around and heads back into the hall. My legs, however, seem to have forgotten how to move.

Her words play on repeat inside my brain.

Did she really just say all those things?

Mood swings … unpleasant … never-ending rude comments …

Slowly, I force my feet to follow her. I'm pretty sure she's never spoken to anyone else like that before. Ever. The knowledge that I'm the one who forced her to act that way makes my stomach turn sickeningly. Does she really think I want to throw up all over her happiness? Of course I don't want to do that. Just because my happiness level is low these days doesn't mean I want that for anyone else.

"Everything okay?" Caleb asks.

I look up and force myself to bite back the 'None of your damn business' retort I'd like to give him.

Be friendly. Pretend you're having a good time. I can do that, right? It's only one week. One week of pretending. If it'll help give my sister the happy day she's been planning for so long, then I can do it. No matter how silly I find the whole thing.

"I—yes." I give Caleb a faint smile and step closer as the music begins playing once again. "Everything's fine." I rest one hand on his shoulder and place the other in his raised palm. Looking firmly over his shoulder at Lucille and Aiden, I prepare to say as little as possible for the remainder of the evening.

"Walk, walk, side, tap," Lucille instructs. "Everyone following? Walk, walk, side, tap."

Caleb and I settle into the rhythm of the simple movement fairly quickly, which he apparently sees as permission to begin a conversation. "Did you get told off by your big sister?"

I glare at him and miss a step. "Just … shh."

He laughs quietly. "Did she tell you to play nicely with me?"

"She told me I could step on your feet as much as I want to," I hiss.

"You, young lady." Lucille snaps her fingers in my direction and steps away from Aiden. "What is your name?"

"This is Sophie," Caleb supplies, giving Lucille his winning smile.

"Sophie, please pay attention," Lucille says. "You are not stepping in time to the music. This is how we do it." She stands behind me, places a hand on either side of my waist, and moves me from side to side in time to the music. My eyeballs send daggers straight at Caleb while he bites his lip and does a terrible job of keeping his laughter in. Lucille doesn't seem to notice. "Yes, like that," she says. "Keep going."

"I might kill you before this lesson is over," I whisper.

"I don't think Sarah would like that."

"And now we try something else," Lucille says. She claps her hands, the music stops, and she pulls Aiden towards her once more. "Now we do the pivot. Watch closely. Walk, walk, pivot, around. Walk, walk, side, tap. Everyone try it with me now. Walk, walk, pivot, around. Walk, walk, side, tap."

Determined not to be told off again, I pay close attention to Lucille and Aiden. Also, it gives me something to look at, since looking at Caleb just makes this whole awkward thing even more awkward. His face is right there and his eyes are right there and I don't want to be *staring into them*. Ugh.

As if he can hear my thoughts, he asks, "Why don't you want to look at me?"

Correction: he can't hear my thoughts, because if he could, he wouldn't need to ask that question. "I have other things to look at."

"Is that so."

"It's weird, okay!"

"Why is it weird?"

As the music starts again, I look at him. Really look at him, at his mouth stretched into a smile, at his eyes—grayish green—and the faint sprinkle of freckles across his cheekbones. "Nope, this is still weird." I look away again.

"It isn't weird, it's fun."

Reluctantly, I take my eyes off the back of the hall and return my gaze to him. His grin is ridiculously large. How can someone smile so wide so often? It can't be real, can it? I shake my head and look away.

"What?"

"Nothing."

"Come on. I know you want to say something."

"You—" I cut myself off and make sure I can say this in the politest, friendliest way possible before continuing.

"Okay, so you're always happy and smiling and enjoying life, right?"

"Right."

"But *this*? All this gushy, soppy wedding stuff? You can't tell me you're actually enjoying this."

Instead of answering my question, his smile stretches a little wider. "I'd like to make a bet with you, Sophie."

"Ugh, no, that is not what I was going for."

"I bet that by the time the wedding arrives, you're going to find yourself enjoying the festivities. You're going to get sucked into the 'gushy, soppy, wedding stuff,' and you'll realise you're having actual, legitimate fun."

I consider his words. "What do I win?"

"Hmm. Anything you want from the craft store."

"Anything?"

"Anything."

"Cool. I'm in."

"Wait, don't you want to hear what I get if I win?" he asks.

"Not really. You're not gonna win." We do the pivot thing for the fourth time, and I wonder if there's another step to be learnt, or if this is it for the world's most boring dance.

"Hey, this isn't gonna work if you're not honest," Caleb says. "When you end up having fun, you have to admit to it."

I raise one eyebrow. "I don't lie."

He raises one eyebrow, mirroring mine in an exaggerated

fashion. "So … don't you want to hear what I'm gonna get *if* I win?"

"Fine. What do you get?"

"I get …" He looks around as he searches for an answer. "A dance with you."

"Dude, you already have to dance with me. That's what this lesson is about, remember?"

"Sure, but this lesson is about you dancing with me *once*. If I win, you have to dance with me again."

"You really want to waste your bet on another dance with me?"

"Well apparently I'm not going to win, so it shouldn't matter what I get, should it?"

I'm almost smiling by now, which is a little disconcerting. "True. Okay, I accept the terms."

The lesson continues, and it turns out that there are in fact no other steps to learn—we don't get to do twirls or dips like Sarah and Aiden—and the dance really is this simple and boring. When the music ends, Lucille waves us to the edge of the hall so she can teach Sarah and Aiden once last step to add to their version of the dance. As Aiden gives Sarah a quick kiss while Lucille is looking the other way, Julia grabs both my wrist and Livi's. She tugs us towards the door and out to the foyer. "Okay, ladies," she says quietly. "We have some bachelorette planning to do."

LuminaireX: Wowee, Wonder Woman. You did a great job on that one, Ash.

AngelSH: Thanks. My boyfriend didn't appreciate it. He was like, why are you drawing pictures of sexy women? That's just weird.

LuminaireX: Good thing my girlfriend doesn't mind when I draw pictures of sexy women :D

AngelSH: No idea if you're joking or not.

LuminaireX: Welllll ... the last girlfriend didn't mind. And the one before that didn't get to see any of my art.

AngelSH: Did she dump your sorry butt too quickly?

LuminaireX: Yep. That's exactly what happened ;)

AngelSH: So anyway, I replied by saying, would you prefer it if I drew pictures of sexy men?

LuminaireX: He he ;)

AngelSH: He wasn't really in a laughing mood, so that conversation ended quickly.

LuminaireX: Hmm. Sorry :(Well, to get back to the point of THIS conversation, your version of Wonder Woman is great. Superhero fans the world over are gonna want prints of it.

AngelSH: Ha ha, somebody already enquired about that actually.

LuminaireX: Awesome! Who says you can't make a living doing what you love ;-)

6

"I THOUGHT WE PLANNED EVERYTHING ALREADY," I SAY AS Julia hurries along a corridor, dragging us behind her.

"Just double-checking we're all on the same page about everything." She tries the handle of the first classroom we come across and finds it unlocked. "It hasn't exactly been easy coordinating everything when the three of us live in different parts of the world." She pulls us inside the classroom and leaves the door ajar.

"This is creepy," Livi says. "We need light." She fumbles against the wall for a few seconds before finding the light switch. The fluorescent tube lights ping and flicker and eventually remain on.

"Okay, let's get down to business." Julia sits and places her phone on the desk in front of her. Livi joins her while I grab a piece of paper and a pen off the front desk. "Oh, you probably won't need to write anything, Soph," Julia adds.

"I know," I say as I slide into a chair opposite her. "The paper's for me."

She taps her phone's screen to find whatever app she keeps her notes in, and I start a rough drawing of a girl in a school dress sitting on … something. I'll decide on that bit when I get there. "Okay, so the kitchen tea picnic is late Monday afternoon," Julia says. "Sarah's arranged to pick up vases for the wedding reception tables from that place in Briardene at four, so we'll have about half an hour from the time she leaves to get everything set up outside. And to get everyone outside waiting to surprise her."

"Half an hour?" Livi said. "Are you kidding? We have to put out blankets and bunting and all the food and drinks and game stuff and music."

"It's fine," Julia says. "We'll get the guys to help before they leave. Oh, and we need to remind everyone not to park in our road otherwise Sarah will know something's up when she gets home." Julia makes a note on her phone. "Cool, so once the kitchen tea is done, Sarah will think all the party stuff is over, and then she'll be super surprised when we take her out on Tuesday evening."

"She's gonna hate it," I say as I add two pigtails with big bows to the little girl's head.

"Sophie," Julia sighs.

"What? I'm not being a downer." I look up for a moment. "I'm being honest. You know she's an introvert to the extreme. She's going to hear the word 'burlesque' and run a mile."

"So don't say the word 'burlesque.' She won't know

what's happening until we get there."

"Right, and *then* she'll run a mile." I return to the drawing, adding a few more lines to the chequered school dress.

"She won't," Livi assures me. "She'll be in the party spirit by then. And we've made this whole event as non-intimidating as we can. Anything embarrassing will happen in front of close friends only."

"Okay." Protruding from the girl's hand, I draw a few lines that will become the stems of a bunch of flowers. "Hopefully you're right."

"Well, well, well. What do we have here?" All three of us look up at the sound of a male voice coming from the doorway. "Still planning?" Caleb says. "Tsk, tsk. The guys are ahead of you in this department. We've had the bachelor event planned for months."

"Our event has been planned for months too," Julia informs him. "We're just ironing out some details. Now shoo." She waves her hand at him. "You're not supposed to know any of this."

"Why? I'm not the bride."

"That isn't the point," Livi says. "Guys aren't supposed to be involved in bachelorette or kitchen tea planning."

"But I can help you make it better."

"I highly doubt that," I say, leaning back and tapping my pen against the page.

"Come on." He pulls a chair out and sits next to me. "I've always wanted to know about the inner workings of bachelorette parties."

His statement is greeted by silence and three sets of raised eyebrows.

"Okay, that was a lie. It's never crossed my mind before. But this seems more interesting than watching the bridal couple stepping on each other's toes."

"No," Livi says. "You need to go back there and make sure Sarah doesn't notice we've left."

"Sarah can't see anything right now beyond the complicated twirly moves Lucille is trying to teach her and Aiden. And if she does notice you're gone, she'll probably think you're doing the girly group toilet visit thing."

"That is so sexist," Livi says.

"And true," Caleb adds—with a grin, of course. "Get on with your planning stuff, and I'll just sit here. Drawing." He reaches for my piece of paper and slides it closer. I'm about to snatch it back, but the memory of Sarah's instruction and her fierce expression make me pause. *You will be friendly, you will keep your never-ending rude comments to yourself, and you will pretend you're having a good time.* I lower both hands into my lap and press my lips together to keep my protest back.

"Cool," Caleb says as he examines the drawing. "Can I add something?"

No, I want to say, but I somehow manage to force the word "Sure" past my lips instead. He reaches for the pen and starts drawing.

"Okay, I've sent a message to the kitchen tea group about not parking right by the house," Julia says, placing her phone back on the desk.

"And I confirmed the final numbers with the burlesque

lady this morning," Livi says.

"Ooh, burlesque," Caleb says as he pushes the drawing back to me. "Kinky."

Livi laughs.

"What is that?" I ask, examining the drawing with a frown. "The girl is supposed to be sitting on a swing, not a dragon."

"Oh, well you didn't mention that. Don't you think sitting on a dragon is more interesting?"

"Yes, but the interesting part was going to be her swinging over an erupting volcano, and the swing was going to be attached to a storm cloud."

"Okay, but now she can fly over a volcano instead."

"Soph, do you still have that sash with the word 'bride' on it from my bachelorette?" Julia asks.

"Uh, yeah, it's in my cupboard." I take the pen and lean over the drawing, finishing the bunch of flowers in the girl's hand with stars on top of the stems instead of petals. Then I move to the dragon's open mouth and draw a stream of stars instead of flames.

"And the bride-to-be alice band?"

"Got that too." I pass the drawing back to Caleb.

"Cool," Julia says. "So the kitchen tea games are sorted, and so is everything for the bachelorette. The cocktails are organized, everyone's on board with the panty game, and—"

"I'll pretend I'm not insanely curious about *that* game," Caleb says as the pen in his hand dances in quick, controlled movements across the page.

"Good, because we're not telling you anything," Livi says.

"I hope you didn't get the penis wand," I say to her. "You know there's no way Sarah's gonna wave that thing around."

"I'm sorry, the what?" Caleb's hand stills over the drawing as he looks up.

"Told you you shouldn't be here," Julia says with a laugh.

"Wait, is that actually a thing?"

"Of course." Livi tries to keep a straight face. "We're getting penis straws too."

Caleb blinks. Then he pushes the drawing back to me. "You're right. I shouldn't be here."

All three of us are laughing—even me—as Caleb makes a swift exit from the classroom. "Well, who knew?" Julia says. "We should have said 'penis' the moment he first sat down."

"Or 'tampon,'" Livi adds with a giggle. "That probably would have worked too."

My smile fades a little as we turn our attention back to checking the final items on Julia's list. She reads them out while I look down at the drawing and see the additions Caleb made: a superhero cape fluttering behind the girl and a mask covering part of her face. A banner at the top of the page says *Dragon Rider Girl*. My smile reappears. Looks like Caleb is capable of more than just boring corporate logos after all.

LuminaireX: Hey, you forgot to title your latest piece.

AngelSH: Oh, oops. Thanks. I'll go back and add something.

LuminaireX: You should call it 'Loneliness.'

AngelSH: What? No. More like 'Blessed Silence.'

LuminaireX: It looks like loneliness.

AngelSH: I can't wait to be alone.

LuminaireX: Really? I can't wait to have a hundred children running around.

AngelSH: OMG. Are you kidding? Have I been messaging a married man all this time? Do you have a pregnant wife who wants to kill me and all the other girls you spend all your time with on Artster?

LuminaireX: Hey, what other girls? You know I have eyes for your art only ;-) (And no, there's no pregnant wife who wants to kill you.)

AngelSH: Thank goodness. Children scare me.

LuminaireX: I was gonna turn the question back on you, but it doesn't quite work with a pregnant husband.

AngelSH: Nope. Thanks for the mental image, though. I'm not freaked out at all now.

LuminaireX: Go to your happy place.

AngelSH: Blessed silence. Got it. I'm there.

LuminaireX: Someone needs to teach you the meaning of HAPPY! :D :D :D

I WAIT IN BED ON SUNDAY MORNING UNTIL THE LAST OF
the pre-church activity is finished and the house is quiet.
Then I pull on a paint-stained T-shirt over my pyjamas and
head downstairs to make something for breakfast. I'm leaning against the counter drinking a glass of water and waiting
for the kettle to boil when I hear someone unlocking the
front door.

"Where did she say she left it?" Caleb asks.

"She couldn't remember," Josh says.

I tap my finger against the side of the glass and wait in
silence. They won't be long. If I'm lucky, they won't even
come in here and I won't have to answer the question, *Why
aren't you joining us for—*

"Oh, hey," Caleb says, appearing in the kitchen doorway.

Not so lucky after all. "Hey. I thought you guys left
already."

"Julia left her purse. She remembered when we reached the end of the road. Apparently she needs it."

"Oh." I look around the kitchen. "Not in here."

"You're not coming with?" Caleb asks.

I'm tempted to say, 'Does it look like I'm coming with?' but I'm supposed to be playing nice. "I don't do the church thing anymore."

"Found it," Josh calls to Caleb from the lounge.

"Okay, coming," Caleb shouts back. "Well, enjoy your morning alone. Don't get too—Oh!"

I see his startled expression at the same moment something thuds onto the counter behind me. It hits the floor, turning out to be a salt shaker. I swing around, already knowing what I'll find: a monkey. It's halfway through the window already, reaching for the fruit bowl someone forgot to move away from the window.

"Hey!" I yell, grabbing the nearest thing—a dishcloth. I snap it at the monkey, now sitting on the inside windowsill, clearly still hoping to make off with a piece of fruit. I throw the towel at the monkey and reach for the empty plastic jug I used to fill the kettle. Before I can throw the jug too, the monkey scrambles away, knocking into the—

"No!" I gasp.

—boxes of miniature jam jars. The top box slides, tilts, and takes a nosedive towards the floor. I lunge, but I'm too late to catch anything. Glass smashes and jam splatters like thick blood across the floor.

"Oh no," I whisper.

75

"Did they believe you?" I ask Caleb as he hurries back into the kitchen. I've got shoes on now, and I'm armed with a bin bag, a newspaper, a window wiper, and a dustpan.

"Told them I'm not feeling well all of a sudden and to go without me."

I shake my head as a crouch down and spread the newspaper open beside the sticky red mess. "Tsk, tsk. Telling lies on a Sunday. You must be losing points for that."

"What, heaven points?"

"Yeah."

Caleb laughs as he bends down. "It actually wasn't a lie. Destroying the bride's special little jam jars from a dear family friend who has now left the country makes me feel kinda queasy."

"It's not a huge deal. We can fix this." I use the plastic edge of the window wiper to start sweeping the mess into the dustpan while Caleb picks out larger pieces of glass and drops them onto the newspaper.

"Look, I'm all for being positive,' he says, "but short of bringing Mrs Govender back from India or breaking into her house and raiding her pantry, how exactly are we going to fix this?"

"We have leftover empty jars because Sarah collected far too many. We just need to get some regular jam and fill each jar. Sarah will never know the difference, and, to be honest, neither will anyone else."

"Sophie Henley," Caleb says, pausing to look at me. "How sneaky of you."

I roll my eyes. "Look, it's the only solution. It saves Sarah from freaking out, and all the guests will get their little thank-you favours."

"It's a good plan," Caleb says. "Do you have any jam lying around, or do we need to go shopping?"

"I'm sure we've got some."

I tip the contents of the dustpan onto the newspaper and continue scooping up the remainder of the sticky glass shards. When we've gathered as much of the mess as possible, Caleb folds the corners of the newspaper over, then rolls it up. "Careful," I say as I hear the crunch of glass.

"Done." He drops the newspaper bundle into the bin bag.

"Thanks. Can you take it to the bin outside the back door, and I'll finish cleaning up."

After wiping the remaining stickiness from the floor with a mop, I check the cupboard for jam. Caleb comes back inside as I finish lining up our options on the kitchen table. "Okay, we've got a big tin that Mom was probably planning to use for baking, a jar that must have come from a food market or something similar, and another jar that Mrs Govender gave us a while back."

"Perfect. Let's start filling."

Several minutes later, we're both sitting at the kitchen table with the empty jars I retrieved from the garage, our supply of jam, and two spoons.

"You know, you're actually quite a pleasant person to be around when you're not trying to be so antagonistic," Caleb says.

Thinking that that's exactly the kind of comment that deserves an antagonistic response, I'm pleased when I manage to say nothing but, "Thanks."

He holds up his first filled jar. "Are these supposed to be sealed in a special way?"

"Um … I don't know."

"I mean, what if the recipients don't open them for months?"

"Then the risk is entirely on them for taking so long to open their lovingly prepared favours."

"Good point. And if something starts growing inside here, hopefully they'll see it."

"Gross," I mutter, screwing the lid onto a jar and moving to the next one.

"So," Caleb says, which I'm pretty sure means he's about to ask me another question. "Everyone else in your family does the church thing, but you don't?"

"Nope."

"Don't you believe in God?"

"Seriously? It is *way* too early in the morning for religion talk."

"I wasn't talking about religion, I was talking about God."

I concentrate on not spilling any jam on the journey from the big tin to the small jar and murmur, "You're just like the rest of my family, aren't you."

"What, we're all a bunch of hippy God-lovers?"

"Yes." I return my spoon to the tin and look at Caleb. "What's wrong with you people?"

"Uh …"

"All this crap happens in the world, yet you insist on believing in an all-powerful, all-loving entity. What about crime and corruption and senseless deaths and—" I almost blurt out Braden's name, but I manage to stop myself. "And—and other tragedies? And don't give me my mother's weak speech about it all being part of 'God's great plan for our lives.' People getting blown up by other people doesn't sound like a great plan. Rape and murder aren't great plans." *Giving your whole heart to someone and finding out it means absolutely nothing to them isn't a great plan either.*

Caleb slowly twists a lid onto the jar he's just filled. "What about free will?"

"Oh, fantastic. The free will argument. That just makes everything better."

"It's not meant to make anything better." He sets the jar aside and looks at me. "It just is what it is. You can't have things both ways. Do you want a perfect world or do you want free will?"

I look away from him and pick up the next empty jar. "This is a stupid argument."

"I thought we were having a discussion."

"Then this is a stupid discussion."

"You believe in *something*, right? Something greater than yourself?"

"Why are we still talking about this?" I grab the spoon

and scoop more jam from the tin. "And no, maybe I don't believe that. Maybe I believe there's just *this* and then there's nothing."

"Firstly, that's super depressing. And secondly, you told me the universe texted you. Therefore you must believe in some Higher Power Universe Thing."

I look at him over the top of the jar. "You know I was just trying to get rid of you when I said that, right?"

"Yes, but it was your first reaction. Which means that deep down, you believe that *something* saved you from me at just the right moment." He gives me a great big grin, as if he's just won the argument.

"Did it?" I ask. "You're still here, aren't you?"

"Okay, I'm rethinking the comment about you being pleasant."

"You're the one who started a conversation about religion and God."

He laughs—and it irritates the heck out of me.

"Just get back to filling the jars, okay?"

"Yes, ma'am," he says.

We fill another few jars in silence, and it isn't long before Sarah's outburst once again comes to mind. Even though she isn't here to witness my unpleasantness, guilt starts creeping up on me. "I'm sorry," I murmur to Caleb.

His hands pause. "You're … sorry?"

"Yes. Look, I may not be interested in interacting with new people, but I don't want to ruin my sister's happiness. So if she wants me to act friendly and polite, then … well, I'm trying. So I'm sorry for being unpleasant."

"Why aren't you interested in interacting with new people?"

Now that part I'm definitely not explaining. "I'm just not. I'm happy on my own. I'm going to go live somewhere beautiful and keep making art. And in between, I'll travel. Visit all the beautiful places in the world and paint them."

"On your own?"

"Yes. As soon as I can afford it. Which, now that I have the time to take on more projects and build my portfolio and start charging more, won't be long."

"What about … friends, family, boyfriend? You'll get lonely."

"I won't be lonely, I'll be *alone*. There's a difference. And I'm not interested in having a boyfriend. Romantic relationships aren't for me." I sort my jars into neat rows and grab the next empty one.

With a chuckle, Caleb says, "I guess you don't know what you're missing out on until you've had one."

"Trust me, I know exactly what I'm missing out on, and I'm happy to give the heartbreak a miss for the rest of time. No more boys for me. Ever."

"Sounds like there's a story behind that statement."

"There is."

When I don't continue, he says, "Well?"

"Doesn't mean I'm going to tell you the story."

"Fiiiiine," he says, drawing the word out on a long sigh. "Okay, the jars are finished. Do we have enough?"

I count the rows we've lined up. "Yeah, that's fine. We

lost twenty-one jars, I think, and we've got twenty-eight here."

"Excellent. We've saved the bride from additional stress."

"While we're at it—and to save the bride from even *more* stress—we may as well start sticking all the thank-you labels on."

"Is that a good idea if the bride isn't here for quality control? What if we stick the labels on crooked?"

"Why would we do that? Aren't you old enough to stick a label on straight, Caleb?"

"Are you being unpleasant again, Sophie?"

I stand up with a sigh and say, "Just teasing."

I fetch the box of printed labels from Sarah's room and return to the kitchen. "Once the labels are on, are the favours finished?" Caleb asks as we begin peeling the stickers from their sheets and carefully placing them onto the side of each jar.

"Nope. We still have to put a piece of hessian over the lid and tie string around it."

"Wow. That's a lot of work for just this one small thing."

"Duh. This is a wedding. A lot of work goes into everything." And it's all a waste of time, in my opinion, but I'm pretty sure that kind of statement falls into the category of 'never-ending rude comments,' so I keep it to myself.

"This isn't a criticism," Caleb says carefully.

"Oh dear."

"It's an honest question." He gets up and fetches a box of label-less jars from the counter. "All this wedding stuff has Sarah quite stressed out. The dress and the favours, all the other things she has to pick up from various people, and I heard her organizing to meet your mother's friend for flower arranging at the venue the day before the wedding. I'm not an expert, obviously—"

"Obviously."

"—but can't you hire people to do all this? I mean, both my parents have been married several times, and neither of them did any of this stuff. Wouldn't Sarah be far more chilled if someone else was taking care of all of this?"

"Well, sure, but that costs a lot more."

"Of course. Right. Sorry." He shakes his head. "I'm an idiot sometimes."

I smile at that. "It's okay. You can't be expected to know everything. The venue Sarah and Aiden chose is super expensive to hire, but they fell in love with it or whatever—" I remember some soppy story about this supposedly gorgeous place "—so that means they had to compromise on other stuff. DIY decor and flowers. Which will still look lovely, I'm sure. It's just more work."

"And more stress."

"Which we're helping to alleviate right now."

"Yes. Go team!" He holds his hand up for a high five.

I eye it with a doubtful expression. "Really? I'm not sure I can fake that much excitement."

"Come on, don't leave me hanging."

"I'm leaving you hanging."

"Nooooo!" He pats the side of my head with his palm. "That'll have to do."

"Wow, you have *no* idea about personal space, do you?"

"Nope. All I know is that you have to pretend to be nice to me, so I'm taking full advantage of that." He gives me a cheshire cat grin. I stick my tongue out at him.

The rest of the label-sticking operation passes by in mostly amicable conversation. We're almost finished when I hear the sound of the gate opening. "Oh, I need to come up with an explanation for my quick recovery," Caleb says.

"And I need to shower. Can you finish up here?"

"Sure. And I'll let everyone know it was your excellent company that got me feeling better so soon."

"Ha! No one's gonna believe that." I hurry upstairs and grab some clothes, hoping to make it back down to the bathroom before anyone sees me. Sarah catches me at the bottom of the stairs, though.

"Hey." Her smile is uncertain. "I just wanted to, um, say how sorry I am for the things I said last night at the dance lesson. I don't know what came over me." She presses both hands to either side of her face. "I ... I don't think I've ever spoken to anyone like that. I'm so sorry."

My eyebrows pinch together. "Why are you sorry? Everything you said was true. I'm supposed to be helping you and making you feel like the special bride that you are, not ruining your wedding with my grumpiness."

"But you have been helping me. You went and got all the wedding favours when I couldn't do it myself. And now you've put all the labels on. And even if you hadn't done anything, I still shouldn't have spoken to you like that. I shouldn't have been so ... bridezilla."

I smile at the word we've so far been unable to apply to Sarah. "You did go a little bridezilla on me, but it was refreshing. You're too nice sometimes."

She groans. "The closer we get to the wedding, the less likely that is to be a problem. And thanks for making an effort with Caleb. Aiden told me you guys got off to a bad start. A misunderstanding in the craft store or something?" She raises her eyebrows in question. "Anyway, he's really not such a bad guy."

"Yeah, I know. I'm the difficult one, not him."

"Don't be silly," Sarah says, pulling me into a brief hug. "You're only difficult some of the time," she adds with a laugh. "And I know you have your reasons. I'm sorry I was so insensitive last night."

I brush her words aside with a shrug as she steps back. She walks away, and I head for the bathroom, and the words that go unsaid are that I actually appreciated her insensitivity. Everyone has spent so long walking on eggshells around me that I'd forgotten what it feels like to be told off for something.

If nothing else, Sarah's insensitivity woke me up.

AngelSH: I am SO in love with that pegasus painting you uploaded yesterday. (Read: jealous of your mad skills.)

LuminaireX: Ash! Hello :D Are your ears burning, cos I was just looking at your gallery.

LuminaireX: Wait, the ears burning thing is when people TALK about you, right? So that doesn't really make sense ...

LuminaireX: ANYWAY, wanted to ask you about that last one ... Does it mean what I think it means?

AngelSH: Well I don't know what you're thinking, but yeah. Probably. I think it kinda speaks for itself, doesn't it?

LuminaireX: So ... the girl in the picture looks sad. She's sitting on the edge of her bed getting dressed in a onesie thingy that looks exactly like her, except the onesie version is smiling. So ... it's like her mask, right? She's depressed, but she covers that up with a smile and no one knows the sad version of her is hiding underneath?

AngelSH: Yep. No hidden meaning there.

LuminaireX: Is that how you feel?

AngelSH: Me? No. Of course not.

LuminaireX: Hey, I get it. I'm just a weirdo on the other side of the Internet. But, you know … we message almost every day now. I kinda feel like you're a friend. If you want to talk about anything …

LuminaireX: Ash?

"DISASTER ALERT!" SARAH SAYS, RUNNING INTO THE kitchen on Monday morning. "Melanie somehow managed to double-book for this Saturday, so now she's *cancelling* on me."

"Wait, who's Melanie?" I ask, looking up from my iPad where I've just registered on yet another website that links creative professionals with potential clients. Next step: uploading all my finished projects to the portfolio section of the website.

"The hair and makeup lady. Sonya from work? It's her sister." Sarah places her hands on her hips and starts pacing. "I mean ... this isn't a *huge* disaster, right? We can find someone else. With less than a week to go. Right?" I can tell she's trying her best to sound rational and positive, but her voice is higher than normal, and panic is evident in her eyes.

Julia, the only other person in the kitchen, lowers the

kettle onto the counter and snatches up her phone. "Yes, of course. This is totally fine, Sarah. We must know someone who knows something about hair."

"Ugh, this is a disaster," Sarah moans, covering her face with her hands.

"Hey, no it isn't," Aiden says, hurrying into the kitchen and placing an arm around Sarah.

"Do you have superhuman hearing or something?" I ask. "I thought you guys were watching TV."

Aiden frowns at me and strokes Sarah's hair. "Why do you need a special lady to do your hair and makeup when you do such a great job yourself?"

"Ah, you're so sweet." Sarah turns in his arms and gives him a quick kiss. "And naive. And really not helping right now."

"Ooh, what about Nandi?" Julia says.

"Your friend from high school?" Sarah asks.

Aiden's arms fall to his sides. "Okay, I can see I'm not needed here."

"Oh, thank you, love." Sarah gives Aiden another quick kiss and turns back to Julia. "Does Nan still live around here? I haven't seen her in ages."

"I think she moved to Ballito," Julia says as she scrolls through her phone. "So she isn't too far away."

"Was that your friend who did the modelling?" I ask.

Julia nods as she raises her phone to her ear and walks to the other side of the kitchen. I turn back to my iPad and get started with uploading the images I've got saved on it. I need to update my portfolios everywhere if I'm hoping to get enough new clients to support my plan of leaving home soon. And with Big Sister Julia to the rescue, it sounds like I'm not really needed for Operation: Hair and Makeup.

Sarah restarts her pacing, and I turn to my phone as I wait for my images to upload. My stomach flip-flops at the sight of an Artster notification from Lex. I open the app and read his message.

LuminaireX: Hey, you haven't uploaded anything recently. Still relaxing after exams?

AngelSH: Not really. Just busy with family stuff.

LuminaireX: That time of year, huh? "Santa Claus is comiiiiing to town."

AngelSH: OMG, don't remind me. I haven't bought a single Christmas present yet.

LuminaireX: Oops, I need to get on that too.

"Okay, Nandi can do makeup," Julia says, "but not hair."

"Whyyyyy is this happening to me?" Sarah moans.

"Jeez, it's not like anyone's dying," I mutter as I type, Chat later. Family stuff.

"Who's not dying?" Mom asks as she comes in through the back door with an empty laundry basket in her arms.

"Melanie cancelled. She can't do our hair and makeup. And I don't know how to do that stuff! That's why I hired a professional! Not that Melanie can really be classified as a professional when she managed to book two weddings at the same time. Doesn't she have a schedule?"

"Approaching bridezilla territory again," I murmur, quietly enough that no one hears me.

"Call Livi," Julia tells Sarah. "Maybe she knows someone who can do hair."

"Sophie, isn't Isabelle's aunt a hair dresser?" Mom asks.

"Um … actually, yes." I pick my phone up again and search for Isabelle's number.

"Ugh, I hate that this stuff is important," Sarah says, pacing past me while her hands twist together. "I mean, it shouldn't be, right? It's just hair. Who cares if it isn't done in some super fancy up-do? But then … I think to myself … I want it to look nice. It's the only time I ever get to dress up like a princess, and …" She drops into the chair across from me and half-moans, half-cries. "I can't believe I just called myself a princess." She covers her face again and mumbles, "I just want to be married already."

"Is it okay for me to mention now that weddings suck?" I whisper to Mom as I place my phone against my ear.

Mom frowns. "No."

After a quick phone call to Isabelle, a pause while she contacts her aunt, and then another phone call, I turn to my once-again-pacing sister. "Cool, Isabelle's aunt is happy to do hair for us. Only thing is, she hasn't done any weddings before. Matric dance hairdos, yes, but no weddings. She said she definitely needs to do a practice run on you."

Sarah's face brightens. "Yes. Okay. Let's go now. Can we

go now? Does she have time?"

"Yeah, she said come any time today and she'll fit you in."

Mom tries not to look too relieved as she says, "Why don't you girls go without me? I'll look through all the decor stuff and see if there's anything we still need to borrow or buy." What she actually means is that she'll be getting food ready for the surprise kitchen tea this afternoon. She was whispering earlier this morning about how we might get Sarah out of the house for a few hours, and now the perfect opportunity has presented itself.

"Yes, okay." Sarah turns and examines her pin board. "Oh, and shoes! You girls don't have shoes yet. Crap, how did we miss that?"

"It's fine, we didn't miss that," Julia says. "We were planning to go after lunch, remember? We'll do the hair now, and then shoes."

"Yes, okay. And then you can meet us for a late lunch somewhere, Mom. We can relax for an hour or two."

"Sure." Mom gives Sarah a wide smile that isn't entirely natural. "We'll be back here in time for you to go and pick up those vases, right?"

"Hmm? Oh. Yeah. Man, how do I keep forgetting everything?"

Over Sarah's shoulder, Julia rolls her eyes and mouths something that looks like *Pin board fail.*

We gather purses and keys and stop in front of the TV on the way out. "Um, just remind me what you guys are doing today," Sarah says.

"The swing thing from the top of the stadium," Aiden tells her. "The Big Rush something-or-other."

"Oh yes. Oh my goodness, please don't die." She hugs Aiden.

"That goes for you too," Julia tells Josh.

"Don't worry, I'll keep them both alive," Caleb says, which is hardly comforting, since we all know he'll probably be the first to leap off the top of the stadium.

"Cool, well, we're off then," I say, shepherding my two sisters towards the door. "Hair disaster fix-up and shoe shopping. Yippee!"

And somehow, the words don't even sound sarcastic leaving my mouth.

AngelSH: Hey, sorry I disappeared the other day.

LuminaireX: No, I'm sorry. I was asking you personal questions, which you obviously don't have to answer.

AngelSH: You're right, though. We are friends. I think I talk to you as much as, if not more than, my friends in real life. That should make you a real friend, right?

LuminaireX: I hope so. (And I mean that in a totally friend-like, non-creepy, non-Internet stalker kinda way.)

AngelSH: Are you friends with all the artists you meet online?

LuminaireX: Not everyone. Some people. Those who ask me lots and lots and LOTS of questions.

AngelSH: Hey, I haven't bugged you with questions in ages.

LuminaireX: I know. Maybe you should. Maybe I miss all your questions ;-)

AngelSH: Um … Okay. I know Photoshop pretty well. Will you teach me Illustrator now?

LuminaireX: HA HA! How much time do you have?

WE MAKE IT HOME AFTER SHOE SHOPPING AND LATE lunch with about half an hour to spare before Sarah needs to leave to fetch her vases. Knowing how much there is to get ready the moment she leaves, it's difficult for us to pretend we're relaxed, normal, and preoccupied with other matters. Sarah takes her time lining up all our shoes and fixing something on hers, and I have to stop myself several times from telling her to hurry up and get out of the house.

Eventually she seems to realise what the time is. With more panicked flapping of her hands, she runs to fetch her purse. "Jules, will you come with me?" she asks as she dashes back through the lounge. Julia looks up at me with wide eyes. I open my mouth, but I can't think of an excuse good enough, and apparently neither can she.

"Um, sure." She stands, mouths *I'm sorry* to me, and hurries outside after Sarah.

The moment Sarah's car turns out of the driveway, we're all hands on deck. Mom grabs her phone and calls Livi to tell her to get her butt inside—in more polite Mom language—then starts replying to texts from the ladies who've already arrived and are waiting in their cars further up the street. I push my iPad aside and run into Dad's study where all the picnic blankets we've borrowed recently have been hiding. By the time I get outside with the bundle of blankets, Aiden, Caleb and Josh have already moved two tables onto the grass. One for snacks and drinks, and the other for gifts. I lay the blankets out on the grass as quickly as I can, while Livi runs outside with bunting streaming behind her. "Go, go, go, guys!" she squeals.

"Need help?" Caleb asks her.

Together they hang the bunting while I help Mom carry glasses and drinks outside. The tables fill up with platters and gifts as our guests arrive. Aunts, cousins, family friends, work friends. After the food, drinks and gifts are arranged, we add the bits and pieces for various games to the tables. Lastly, we arrange the outdoor furniture around the edge of the blankets for the ladies who feel a little bit too old to get down on the ground.

Livi stands back, examines the picnic area, and says, "I think everything's done, actually. Wow. That was impressive."

"Fantastic team work," Mom says. "Well done, everyone."

I check my phone as it buzzes. "Jules just messaged," I tell everyone. "They'll be home in five minutes."

"Okay, we're off," Aiden says.

"Where are you guys spending the afternoon?" I ask, wondering for the first time if Josh and Caleb might possibly have planned Aiden's bachelor party for this evening. They don't exactly have many days left before the wedding.

"That pub in Davallen Avenue," Aiden says. "The Taphouse. Your dad's meeting us there when he's finished at work."

I look over at Josh and Caleb to see if they're exchanging secretive glances, but their eyes give nothing away. "Cool. Enjoy," I tell them.

They head off, and everyone else gathers together on the picnic blankets. I hover inside near the front door, checking the window continuously for Sarah's car. The moment the gate starts opening, I dash back through the house to the garden, noticing all of a sudden that I'm actually finding all surprise business quite fun. "They're here, they're here!"

A hush falls over the gathering, with only one or two stifled giggles and whispers disturbing the quiet. I hear Sarah and Julia chatting inside. Through the open door, I see them lowering boxes onto a table. Sarah's right there, a step or two away from the door, and somehow she hasn't seen us yet. Then she turns and—

"SURPRISE!"

"Oh my goodness," she gasps, clapping one hand to her chest and the other to the arm of the couch. I can't help joining in the roar of laughter. Looking utterly shocked, Sarah lets Julia take her arm and lead her outside. Finally, she starts laughing—and that gets everyone started all over again.

As the afternoon continues with gift guessing, recipe collecting, a game of bridal bingo, and dressing Sarah in a toilet paper wedding gown, that tiny spark of joy within me doesn't diminish. As crazy as it sounds, I think I may be in danger of losing this bet with Caleb.

ARTSTER APP

1 year, 1 month, 7 days ago

LuminaireX: Did someone get kissed in the rain recently? ;-)

AngelSH: Nope. Someone wished she got kissed in the rain, but someone's boyfriend thinks it's silly to stay outside and get wet when it starts raining.

LuminaireX: Is someone talking about herself in the third person?

AngelSH: Maybe :P

AngelSH: Anyway, what do you think of the piece? Is it any good?

LuminaireX: Any good? AngelSH, that piece is going to make girls all over the world wish they were being kissed in magical rain by a boy who looks just like that.

AngelSH: You can't really see much of the boy …

LuminaireX: I'm trying to tell you your artwork is amazing.

AngelSH: Right, thank you. I think I'm finally getting the hang of the mixer brush.

LuminaireX: What do you mean? You got the hang of it ages ago.

AngelSH: I mean it's getting easier.

LuminaireX: Excellent :D

LuminaireX: I'm thinking of an old song …

LuminaireX: Found it! Perfect for you. Kiss the Rain :D

AngelSH: LOL. Got it already. It was on repeat while I was drawing.

LuminaireX: Ha ha! You really like this kissing in the rain idea.

AngelSH: *shrug* A silly, girly idea, but it seems romantic.

LuminaireX: Until you end up choking on all the rain.

AngelSH: But if your lips are attached to someone else's, how is the rain getting into your mouth?

LuminaireX: Since when are my lips involved in this scenario?

AngelSH: Not YOUR lips, idiot. You know what I mean. Okay, I guess some rain is going to get in your (not YOUR) mouth, but not a lot. Not enough to choke you.

LuminaireX: What if it's a heavy downpour?

AngelSH: Then I probably won't be outside anymore.

LuminaireX: What if it's a monsoon?

AngelSH: Stop ruining my kiss in the rain.

Half the ladies have left and the remainder are lounging on the picnic blankets as Livi and I carry glasses and plates inside and get started on washing up. My phone vibrates in my pocket while I'm busy loading the dishwasher, but I manage to keep from checking it until I'm done.

LuminaireX: Remember I told you about VAU Art Con? The one being held in Rome next year? And how there was a competition for people to win tickets?

Smiling to myself, I take a seat at the kitchen table while Livi heads back outside.

AngelSH: Yes, yes and yes.

LuminaireX: Guess what? I won two tickets!

AngelSH: That's awesome! Does two tickets mean for two days? Two panels? Two events?

LuminaireX: No, silly. Two tickets means two people for the whole thing. Cos who wants to go to something like this alone ;-) I thought you might be able to go. We could meet up there.

We could *meet up there*? I lean back in my chair and bite my thumbnail. What am I supposed to say to that? Lex and I have gone almost two years without either of us ever suggesting we meet. I kinda thought we could go on like that forever.

AngelSH: Oh ...

LuminaireX: Oh? That's all I get? I offer you the artistic opportunity of a lifetime, and all I get is 'oh'???

AngelSH: Artistic opportunity of a lifetime might be an overstatement. And it's too far away for me.

LuminaireX: Oh :-(Where would you have to fly from?

AngelSH: Why does it matter?

LuminaireX: It doesn't, I guess. Just wondering how far away it is for you.

AngelSH: Too far.

LuminaireX: Which means?

AngelSH: Are you asking me where I live?

LuminaireX: Yeah. I already know a thousand random facts about you. Seems odd I don't know where you live. And you don't know where I live either.

AngelSH: That's fine. It's not like it matters.

LuminaireX: I get the feeling you don't actually want to tell me.

AngelSH: Maybe I don't. Maybe I don't want Internet people knowing where I live.

LuminaireX: ???

LuminaireX: Seriously? 'Internet people?' I thought we were friends.

"Ugh, Sophie, you idiot," I mumble, rubbing my hand over my face. "That was *not* the right thing to say."

AngelSH: Yeah, but I still don't actually KNOW you.

LuminaireX: You're kidding.

AngelSH: I'm not kidding.

Why is he making this a big deal? This doesn't have to be a big deal. It shouldn't be a huge revelation to either of us that we don't actually *know* each other in real life.

LuminaireX: We've been friends for almost two years, and suddenly you think I'm an Internet weirdo?

AngelSH: I didn't say that.

LuminaireX: You didn't have to.

AngelSH: Lex ...

I bite my lip, waiting for his reply, but it doesn't come.

AngelSH: Lex!

LuminaireX: What?

AngelSH: Can't we just keep this ... here? As it is? Online?

LuminaireX: I wasn't asking you to marry me. It's just an art con. Just two friends meeting up.

AngelSH: I know.

I just about chew a hole through my lip while waiting for him to reply. He doesn't.

AngelSH: Lex?

LuminaireX: Sure, Ash. We can keep it online.

I don't have a clue what else to say now, so I end up saying nothing. My insides clench sickeningly. Lex has never been upset with me before. He's always sunshine and happiness, a constant force I can count on to pull me from the darkness if I ever find myself lost in it. Braden used to get moody sometimes because of me. Moody, annoyed, upset—and then he'd break up with me. And I'd be crushed and broken, wondering if this time it really was the end.

Echoes of past hurts bounce around my chest, making it ache. What if Lex breaks·up with me? What if I've upset him so much that he decides to end our Internet friendship? Dammit, why did he have to ask about this stupid art con thing?

An ache behind my eyes alerts me to the fact that tears are on the way. I blink and breathe deeply in and out. I don't cry anymore. I did enough crying a year ago to last me a lifetime. When I finally stopped, I stopped for good.

I stand and look out the kitchen window. I can't go back outside now. No way. I can't be happy and chatty and excited. I'll probably lash out with some rude comment, and I'll end up making things *unpleasant* for everyone. Again.

Instead, I climb the stairs to my room. I close the door behind me—and turn to find Sarah sitting on the floor hugging one of my pillows. "Hey, sorry," she says, smiling up at me. "I'm just hiding for a little bit. So many people … it gets a bit much after a while, so I just need to recharge in quiet for a few minutes."

I clear my throat so my voice doesn't come out sounding wobbly and emotional. "Yeah, okay."

"I mean, I loved it," she adds quickly. "I really did. Thank you so much for everything you guys have done."

"Sure." I lower myself to the floor opposite her. "We know you love all the gooey, happily-ever-after crap."

She raises an eyebrow.

"Sorry." I breathe out a long sigh, hoping to rid myself of the sick, twisting feeling in the pit of my stomach. "I'm sure all the happy love stuff will work out great for you and Aiden."

She gives me a wry smile. "You're a bad liar, Sophie Henley."

"Look, it's not that I don't believe people can find their soulmate and live happily ever after. I just don't believe it for *me*." Apparently I can't even keep friends for longer than a few years. Lex is already distancing himself from me.

The sick feeling gets worse.

"Soph," Sarah says quietly. "What happened with Braden … that isn't going to happen again."

"Yeah. Well, not *exactly* like that. But the end result will be the same, and I'm just not interested in going through that again."

"Come on, Sophie. You're only eighteen. You can't possibly—"

"Yes, and I'm perfectly happy going through the rest of my years without any more heartbreak. I've had enough to last me a lifetime."

"I know. I get it. Nobody should have to go through what you went through with Braden. I'm just saying that you're missing out on so much happiness by shutting out the possibility of ever—"

"Stop, Sarah," I snap. "Just stop. I don't need a great romance in my life to make me happy."

"Fine, sorry," she says, her eyes widening as she raises her hands. "We can talk about me instead, and how I'm freaking out about the decor and rehearsal dinner and the honeymoon and … you know." Her cheeks grow pink. "The first night."

Because I'm hateful and hurting and want someone else to feel worse than I do, I let my eyebrows climb up my forehead and say, "You and Aiden haven't slept together yet?"

Mild surprise crosses her face. "No, of course not."

"Wow. So you guys clearly have zero physical attraction to one another."

Since she's stuck in that horrid lovey dovey place where

my insults can't reach her, she starts smiling instead of getting offended. She buries her face in the pillow for a moment and mumbles, "I think it's called superhuman restraint."

"I don't know what you're getting so nervous about. Sex is overrated." She looks up with a small frown. I focus my gaze on a paint stain on my shorts. "Awkward, uncomfortable … *messy*. I doubt a clean freak like you will enjoy it." *Stop it, Sophie. Just stop, stop, stop being so hateful.* But I can't. Sometimes the darkness inside me spills out and gets on other people.

"Did you and Braden …"

"Yeah." I half shrug. "Of course. No big deal." She knows I'm lying. She knows it was a big deal.

"Does Mom know?"

I roll my eyes and meet Sarah's wide-eyed gaze. "Why would I tell Mom that my boyfriend and I were sleeping together when I'm supposed to be a good girl who waits for marriage? Like I'd really want to give her another reason to be disappointed in me."

"Soph … she isn't disappointed in you. She just worries about you. And everyone makes mistakes, so she can't judge you for yours."

"Who says it was a mistake?" I lean back on my hands, covering up my broken, hurt interior with a casual exterior. "I don't hold your silly beliefs about waiting. I wanted to have to sex." *Braden* wanted to have sex. I thought it would make him happy and bring us closer. And I kind of wanted to. It's not like he forced me.

"So you don't regret it?" Sarah asks. "You don't wish you'd waited?"

"No, I don't regret it." I do regret it. I wish I'd waited. For someone else. For someone worth it. Which is kinda sad, considering I don't believe that person exists. Not for *me*.

"I'm sorry," Sarah says quietly. Because, like she said, I'm a bad liar and she knows the truth.

"Stop being sorry!" I shout, my carefree pretense gone in an instant. "You're always *sorry* about something. Always over-apologetic. This has nothing to do with you. My relationship with Braden never had anything to do with anyone else, so everyone needs to stop being *sorry*."

Sarah sets the pillow aside and stands. "I can't deal with you when you're like this," she says quietly. "You want to pull everyone down with you, but I'm not letting you do it this time. I won't let you make me feel bad for being happy." She leaves my room, closing the door quietly behind her.

I squeeze my eyes shut and press my lips together and force myself to *breathe*. I hate, hate, hate myself for the things I've said. I hate myself for being so selfish that I can't keep my hurt inside. And I hate that Lex has come to mean so much to me that a disagreement with him can upset me this much. Or was it the fact that Sarah and I started speaking about Braden? That our conversation dug up memories of … everything. Is that why my chest feels like it's just been ripped open?

I climb onto my bed and draw my knees up to my chest.

I press my hands over my eyes. "Don't cry, don't cry, don't cry," I murmur as I focus on breathing slowly in and out.

A knock at my door startles me. I lower my hands, but say nothing. If it was Sarah, she would come back in without knocking, and I'd say how sorry I am over and over again. But it isn't Sarah, and I don't want to speak to anyone else.

The knock comes again. "Sophie?" It sounds like Caleb, but his voice is muffled enough that I can't be sure. I remain silent, waiting for him to—

The door opens. "Oh, hey, you are here," Caleb says when he sees me. "We just got home, and your mom sent me to ask if—"

"You *opened the door*?" I demand. Who the hell does that without being invited in?

"Well, you didn't answer, so …" His words trail off as his gaze slips past me to the wall. To the art covering almost every part of my room.

"Yeah, that generally means *don't* come in," I tell him.

He doesn't answer. I'm not sure he even heard me. He's still staring at the walls, his eyes travelling slowly from piece to piece.

"Hey!" I yell, trying to pull his attention away from the art. It's my soul that's plastered up there, and I don't like the way he's gawking at it. "Will you please leave?"

"I …" His gaze is stuck on something. I don't want to look at which one it is. Something he finds disturbing, based on his expression. And that hurts, because for some reason I *want* him to like what he sees.

"Hey!" I shout again. "If you don't like what you see, then *stop looking*."

"I ..." He still can't seem to pull his eyes from my paintings. "I didn't say that."

"You didn't have to. Your face says it all perfectly clearly."

"My face isn't—"

"Just get out!" I yell, grabbing the nearest cushion and throwing it at him.

He backs away and tugs the door shut as the cushion hits the wall.

AngelSH: Do you ever feel like you're about to fall off the edge? Like you're standing at the brink of a great, dark pit, and all these demons are writhing around at the bottom, reaching up for you with clawed hands, and you know if they could get hold of you, they'd pull you under completely. You're safe if you keep standing. If you keep out of the pit. But you're so tired and you just don't have the strength to keep upright, and all you want to do is let go and fall, fall, fall into the darkness. Or maybe you're already falling and you can't remember the moment when you let go. You're falling in slow motion, with the demons getting closer and the darkness getting darker.

AngelSH: I want to draw that but I don't have the energy.

AngelSH: Maybe I'm not falling yet. I'm not sure. But I'm standing right at the edge, looking down, and something is coming. I just know it. Something's coming, and it's going to push me off the edge.

* * *

AngelSH: I'm sorry. I wish there was a delete button. I went outside and breathed some fresh air and realised you SO did not need to know all that. It was just … a dark moment.

* * *

LuminaireX: Hey, what's going on, Ash? Are you okay? I'm sorry I didn't reply earlier. Battery died while I was out.

LuminaireX: Hello, hello, hello?

LuminaireX: You know, it's kinda not so cool when you tell someone you might be about to fall into a dark demon pit, and then … you stop replying to messages. Just saying. You should reply now. If only to tell me to shut up.

LuminaireX: Ash?

I NEED TO GET OUT OF THE HOUSE. I DON'T CARE THAT darkness is growing closer and it isn't safe. I slip outside the front without anyone noticing—not a difficult feat when everyone's chilling in the back garden with the remaining kitchen tea guests—and head along the road.

I find it easier to breathe out here. My head is clearer and my heart isn't as heavy. The Braden-sized hole in my chest begins to close again. I still feel horrid for all the things I said to Sarah, and scared that Lex won't ever reply to my messages again, but at least my chest doesn't feel ripped open. Braden is in the past. I've worked hard to leave him there. Now I need to work hard at not letting conversations about him cause me to feel so raw.

I'm several houses away from Isabelle's when I start freaking out. It's almost completely dark now, and I can see someone walking slowly towards me from the other end of the road. Someone who probably has no plans to hurt me in any way, but what if I'm wrong? What if today is the day I get mugged or worse? It's stupid and paranoid, but I run straight for Isabelle's house and press the buzzer the moment I get there. The dark figure up ahead hasn't changed his pace, so I'm most likely panicking for no reason.

"Hello?" says the disembodied voice through the intercom box.

"Hi, um, it's Sophie."

After a pause, the gate starts wheeling open. I hurry inside faster than necessary. I cross the driveway to the front door, which opens to reveal a surprised Isabelle. "Sophie? What are you doing here?"

"Um … not ignoring you?" I glance over my shoulder as the gate slides shut.

"Great. Come on in." She shuts the door after I've walked inside, then takes a closer look at me. "Is everything okay?"

"Yeah, I just …" I breathe out as my heart rate returns to normal. "There are just a lot of people at home right now. I needed a break, that's all."

"Well I'm happy you chose to come here," she says with a smile, which leaves me feeling guilty since I only ran to her house because it was closer than mine.

As we reach Isabelle's bedroom, my phone starts ringing. Mom's face shows up on the screen, and another shot of guilt rushes through me. "Hi, Mom."

"Soph, where are you?" she asks, her tone just a tiny bit

anxious. "No one can find you."

"I'm at Isabelle's."

"Oh, okay." Mom's relief is obvious. "I'm sorry, I must have forgotten you said you were going there. We're ordering pizzas, so I wanted to check what you'd like. Will you be back for supper?"

"I, uh, actually forgot to tell you I was coming here. I'm sorry." Total lie, but Mom will only worry more if I tell her I was so upset I just walked out. "And I'll be with Isabelle's family for supper—" I throw a questioning glance at Isabelle to confirm, and she nods vigorously "—so you don't need to order me anything. But thank you."

I know I should go home and apologise to Sarah and Caleb, but I'm too embarrassed now to face either of them. Perhaps if I wait a few hours, that embarrassment will magically disappear. Doubtful, but I can hope.

"We're also doing takeout," Isabelle says after I end the call with Mom. "Well, we're going for a stroll along the promenade, then getting takeout."

"Sounds great."

"Awesome!" She plops onto her bed and leans down to put her shoes on. "Several entire hours in which you can't fake an excuse to escape from me. Whatever shall we talk about?"

"Uh …"

"Will you kill me if I bring up the subject of Braden?"

Seriously? She had to lead with that?

"O-kay," she says slowly, looking up at my expression. "Maybe not Braden."

My gaze drops to the tiny star below my thumb. Then my right hand slides over it, forcing me to look elsewhere. "It's just that it's in the past, you know? So what's the point in talking about him?"

"Sure," Isabelle says, smiling and nodding as she returns to tying her shoelaces. But I can tell she doesn't agree.

LuminaireX: Just checking in again. I think this is check-in message #4 …

LuminaireX: Sorry if I'm annoying you. You should tell me if I am. Tell me to piss off. I won't be offended.

AngelSH: Hi

LuminaireX: Ash! Are you okay?

AngelSH: Yes.

LuminaireX: Really? Not sure I believe that one …

AngelSH: I mn

AngelSH: I'm not gonna be online for a while.

LuminaireX: Are you … falling off the edge?

AngelSH: Thanks for your daily check-in messages. I'm sorry I worried you. You don't have to check in anymore.

AngelSH: xx

LuminaireX: Okay, now I definitely don't believe that everything's okay with you.

LuminaireX: Look, you obviously don't have to tell ME what's going on, but you have someone else to talk to, right? Someone in real life?

LuminaireX: Hello?

LuminaireX: Ash?

Hanging out with Isabelle, her parents and her younger brother almost makes me feel like I'm living my former life. My life when Iz and I went to the same school, hung out with the same friends, shared secrets, and giggled about boys.

Almost, but not quite.

When Isabelle's dad drops me off at my gate, that twinge of anxiety is still there. As the gate rattles closed behind me and I walk towards the house, I check my phone to see if Lex has sent a message in the past few hours. I find plenty of Artster notifications from followers liking my art, but not a single notification about a private message. My heart sinks a little further.

Once inside the house, I peek around the lounge door and find the room in semi-darkness with everyone staring at the TV. Looks like I missed family movie night. I hang out in the hallway, checking emails on my phone while leaning against a section of the wall where I can see into the lounge.

When Caleb stands and heads to the kitchen with several empty glasses in his hands, I dart through the lounge, waving quickly at everyone, and into the kitchen. Caleb places the empty glasses on the counter and turns to the fridge. With his hand raised towards the fridge handle, he sees me. "Sophie, hey." He lowers his hand. His perpetual smile is still present, but it doesn't seem as wide as normal, and there's definitely a wariness in his tone. Probably afraid I'll throw something at him again.

"Hi. So, uh, I wanted to apologize for, um …" A quick glance over my shoulder tells me we're still alone in the kitchen. "For yelling at you. And throwing a pillow at you. Not particularly mature on my part, I know, but I was upset. About something else."

Caleb nods, watching me carefully and, for once, not saying anything else.

"Anyway, I need to apologise to Sarah too. I've been supremely bitchy today, and she didn't deserve it."

Caleb's eyes widen a tad in question.

"Nope, sorry, I will not be repeating the things I said. Um, yeah, so I'm gonna go chat to her now."

It looks as though Caleb may be about to say something, but I don't hang back to hear it. This conversation feels awkward enough as it is.

I cross the lounge and sink into the tiny space next to Sarah. My phone buzzes in my hands, and when I turn it over, I see an Artster notification of a private message. Icy nervousness rushes through me as I open the message.

LuminaireX: Ash! You know that book cover we were gushing over last month? The illustration with all the tiny birds that made up a black and white cityscape? Well that illustrator just won this year's Marg-Evans Award for Best Cover Design. We totally predicted that :D

Warmth spreads throughout my insides, and a smile pulls my lips up. I don't know why, but Lex seems to have forgotten he was upset with me earlier. Or maybe this is the way normal people act. They get upset, then get over it. Not like Braden, who used to cling to his hurt as it dragged him—and me, sometimes—down into the dark depths. I bite my lip and turn the phone back over. I'll reply later when I get into bed.

I turn my attention to the movie. After watching it for a few moments, I nudge Sarah's hand with mine and curl my pinkie finger around hers. "I'm sorry," I whisper. "I'm really, really sorry. I didn't mean anything I said earlier."

She squeezes my finger with hers, tilts her head to rest against mine, and whispers, "I know."

And even though I'm lightyears away from deserving it, everything's somehow okay again.

AngelSH: Hey, Lex.

LuminaireX: Ash! You came back :D (You can't see me—obviously—but I'm waving madly at you.)

AngelSH: Yeah. I came back.

LuminaireX: What happened?

AngelSH: Just ... stuff.

LuminaireX: I missed you.

AngelSH: Really? Don't you have a ton of online artist friends?

LuminaireX: Sure, but most of them get bored with all my messages. You let me keep babbling as long as I want ;-)

AngelSH: Maybe I got bored too. Maybe that's why I left Artster.

LuminaireX: That's not why you left.

AngelSH: You're right. It isn't. I'm sorry. You could never make me bored.

LuminaireX: I'm getting the feeling you're not gonna tell me what happened.

AngelSH: I'm getting the feeling you're right.

LuminaireX: I really did miss you.

AngelSH: I missed you too.

A STORM WAKES ME EARLY ON TUESDAY MORNING. I LIE IN
bed and think of when I was little and I'd suffer through
sweltering, sticky summer days at school, only to change out
of my uniform the moment I got home and jump into the
pool. Then I'd spend the afternoon doing homework with
my wet, chlorine-infused hair dripping down my back,
providing temporary relief from the heat. And then finally,
as evening drew closer, clouds would gather, blown in on a
cool breeze, and the sky would take on that oddly luminous
look. Fat raindrops would start to squeeze themselves out of
the clouds and plop down, sizzling on the still-hot concrete.
And *suddenly* the heavens would tear open and unleash a
deluge of water and electricity and house-shuddering
booms. And we'd finally have the relief we'd craved all day.

Just like we used to do then, I count the seconds
between each flash and the responding boom, and as the

storm gets closer, I force myself out of bed and unplug all the important technology in my bedroom. With every cent of my savings going towards my move-away-from-home fund, it would be a major setback if my surge protector plug failed to work and I had to buy a new computer.

After breakfast, when the electrical part of the storm is over, I return to my room and get settled at my computer. I have to finish an illustration for one client, and send drafts to another three, and that all needs to happen before the wedding. Normally, I'd be fine with that, but normally my time is my own and I don't have to play wedding coordinator assistant.

I'm looking through the examples sent to me by one of the newer clients when I hear a quiet tap at my door. "Yes?" I say.

Caleb pokes his head into my room. "You're not gonna throw anything at me, are you?"

"Not this time," I say, smiling at him and finding it a lot easier than I did a few days ago. "Can't make any promises about the future, though."

He chuckles. "So … can I come in?"

"Um, okay."

He steps inside and looks around, schooling his expression into something a little more polite than the gawking he was doing yesterday. "So I see today's an iMac day, not a garage day," he says.

"Yeah, I don't have many garage days."

"Do you have a little studio down there?"

"Not exactly. More like a tiny corner with bad lighting,

no windows, and Dad's shelving fencing me in. Totally the romantic painter image."

"Hey, we can't all be sitting on the streets of Paris wearing a beret and painting the passersby."

"*You* probably could be." I lean my elbows on my desk. "In fact, I'm guessing you've done that already."

He gives me a half-smile. "Sort of." He gestures to my walls as he walks slowly across the room. "I don't dislike any of this, by the way. I think it's amazing, actually."

"I suppose you would, considering you design corporate logos for a living." I slap my hand over my mouth, then slowly lower it. "Crap. Sorry. I'm supposed to keep all my rude comments to myself."

"You may be surprised, Sophie Henley," he says in superior tones, "to hear that I can draw more than just logos."

"Oh, I know, you can draw cartoon dragons too," I say, referencing the pen drawing he added his own elements to in the classroom after the dance lesson.

"Yes. And non-cartoon dragons." He lifts the lightweight wooden chair from the corner of my room and sets it next to mine. "So what are you working on?"

I wheel back slightly to put a bit more distance between us. "Um …" I don't usually share my ideas with anyone before they're executed. I always think they sound silly in words, but once they're drawn on paper, they make more sense. But I guess I kinda owe him after the logo comment. "Well, uh, this author wants me to do a character postcard for the main character from her urban fantasy series." I scoot closer to the desk and nod towards the screen. "She sent me links to a few examples of stuff she likes so I could get a feel for what she wants. The main character's a vampire, so I've obviously gotta show some fangs, and then I was thinking of drawing her in a stance kinda like this one—" I point to one of the examples "—and adding high-rise buildings behind her. Dark, smokey sky. City lights."

"Sounds great," Caleb says. "And the 'swirly glow'?" He points to the notes window open on one side of the computer screen where I've got the list of details the author gave me.

"Oh yeah. She wants it to be obvious that this vampire has magic, so I'm supposed to add a swirly glow—her words—around the vampire's hand."

"Cool. You're good at that kinda thing."

Another compliment? In the same conversation? "Uh … thanks."

"I mean, there's lot of magical stuff all over your walls," he adds quickly, "so I can see you're good at it."

Why can't we stick to insults instead of compliments? They're far less awkward. "Um, anyway, so then the other thing I need to start is a steampunk poster." I navigate to my desktop—the background of which is a painting of a ship, one of my favourites by Lex—and open the folder where I've saved a whole bunch of steampunk inspiration pictures. "The client doesn't want it for anything specific. She just loves steampunk stuff, likes my style of art, and wants a custom illustration to stick up in her house somewhere."

"That's, uh—" Caleb coughs and clears his throat

"—that's really cool. I haven't ever done anything steampunk related, but now that I think about it, it would probably be loads of fun."

"Yeah, so I need to get started on that one asap, because it's gonna be huge and detailed. The biggest thing I've done so far. Which is cool, 'cause it also means I can charge quite a bit more for it."

"How's that going?" Caleb asks. "Your plan to leave home and visit beautiful places in the world and paint them."

I lean back in my chair and tap a pen against my knee. "Not really sure. I've saved quite a bit, but depending on where I want to go when I move out, it may not be enough yet. If I stay in the country it obviously won't cost me nearly as much as going overseas, for example. But I really want to go somewhere new. Fill my creative well with new experiences. So I'll wait a bit longer and save a bit more if that's what it'll take." Wow, I am being *way* too chatty this morning. I blame Sarah and her instruction to 'be friendly.'

"Where are you thinking of going?" Caleb asks.

"You're the intrepid traveller," I say. "Where do you suggest I start my new life?"

"Well, I'll start off by suggesting that you get to know the people in whatever community you find yourself in, instead of insisting on a lonely life."

"It won't be a *lonely* life," I say. "I've already explained that part. It's not as though I'm going to completely ignore the family and friends I already have. I'll keep in contact. I just don't think I need a lot of day-to-day interaction with people. I'm not like that." Because I'll end up getting attached, and then it'll hurt when I have to say goodbye.

"Everyone's like that," Caleb says.

"*You're* like that," I say, pointing my pen at him. "But that doesn't mean everyone else is like that." I spin around on my chair two or three times. "Anyway, you still haven't suggested a destination for me."

"You live in such a beautiful country," he says. "Why do you want to leave it?"

I bring the chair to a stop. My gaze lands on the star tattoo before quickly moving on. *Bad memories*, my mind whispers, but out loud, I say, "There are plenty of beautiful places in the world. I've already seen some of this country, so now it's time to see others. It's time to go adventuring."

"Adventuring is more fun with other people. I should know. I've done it both ways."

"But I'm not you. I want to go on adventures on my own."

He leans forward and rests his elbows on his knees. He watches me closely and says, "I'm not going to be able to convince you otherwise, am I?"

My eyes slide away from him and move to the bottom right corner of my desktop where a portion of Lex's painting is visible amidst all the application windows I've got open. Loop-scribble-loop goes his signature. I could have gone adventuring with him. Around Rome, at least, if I'd agreed to meet him for that art con. But I have my rules. I don't want to get attached and end up heartbroken, and that's why I had to say no.

"No," I say to Caleb, my eyes moving back to his. "You can't convince me otherwise, I'm afraid." I grab hold of the desk and pull myself closer. "And now you need to leave so I can get started on these projects."

"But I want to watch the master at work," Caleb protests. "That's why I came up here."

"No. Definitely not."

"Pleeeeease."

I point to the door. "Go."

He smiles. "Fine."

AngelSH: Did you ever get a tattoo you regretted?

LuminaireX: Ha ha! What's the tattoo?

AngelSH: The problem isn't WHAT it is. The problem is WHO it makes me think of.

LuminaireX: Ah. Yes. I totally get that … Every time I look at the giant rose on my shoulder with my ex-girlfriend's name tattooed over it, I ask myself, why oh why did you ever think this was a good idea?

AngelSH: Now you're just making fun of me.

LuminaireX: Never ;)

AngelSH: Good thing my ex-boyfriend has the same name as the guy I'm currently crushing on.

LuminaireX: Um …

LuminaireX: Really?

AngelSH: No, you idiot. I would never tattoo someone's NAME onto my body. I'm not that stupid.

LuminaireX: Whew. I'm never entirely sure when you're joking.

AngelSH: I've figured out by now when you're joking ;-)
(Answer: almost always)

LuminaireX: :P

ON TUESDAY EVENING—SURPRISE BACHELORETTE NIGHT—
Julia and I try not to give anything away during dinner. I
almost slip up twice, but thanks to a few well-aimed jabs to
the side from my dear older sister, I manage to cover up
what I've said. We sneak away while everyone's cleaning up
in the kitchen and get dressed in my bedroom in party-
appropriate dresses and makeup.

At precisely 7 p.m., the gate buzzer rings. I peek out my
window. "Yep, it's Livi."

"Wow, she's remarkably punctual," Julia says as she
checks her appearance one last time before heading for the
door.

"She probably waited outside until exactly this moment."

As we hurry downstairs, I hear Sarah walking to the front
door. At least, I hope it's Sarah. Everyone was given
instructions about making sure she'd be the one to open the

131

door tonight. "Hi, who's there?" she asks, speaking into the intercom. "Oh, hi, Isabelle. Sure."

Julia chuckles. "Good thing our intercom's so bad you can't tell who's on the other end of it."

We peek into the hallway and watch as Sarah opens the door. "Livi?"

"Surprise!" Livi shouts, and Jules and I run to join her.

"What?" Sarah takes in our sparkly dresses and made up faces. "Oh my goodness. What's happening?"

"What do you think is happening?" Livi says, giving her a wink.

"But we already had a thing yesterday," Sarah protests.

"Yeah, that was to keep all the old ladies happy," Julia says. She gives Sarah a mischievous grin and adds, "Tonight's the real party."

The bride-to-be loses some of the colour in her cheeks.

"Okay, girls, we have ten minutes," Julia says. "Let's get her dressed and ready, and then it's party time!"

"Oh my goodness," Sarah mutters.

"Don't worry," I whisper to her. "You're gonna have fun."

"No," Sarah says when she sees the flashing burlesque sign outside the dance studio. "No way, no way. What are you guys doing to me?" she wails.

"It will be fun, I promise," Julia says as she drags Sarah—

complete in her 'bride' sash and 'bride-to-be' alice band—out of the car. "It's just us and a few of your friends from work and church. Come on, you *know* it isn't going to be bad if we invited church people."

"I hate you," Sarah moans.

I wrap one arm around her as we walk inside. "It's just a class," I tell her. "Like a gym class, but way more fun. We'll put feather boas on and dance around chairs and pretend to be sexy. We'll all look silly together instead of making you do embarrassing things on your own."

"Okay," she murmurs. "I guess that isn't *too* awful."

As we walk into the dance studio, the rest of Sarah's friends yell "Surprise!" and rush forward to hug her. They've already got their feather boas on, and they make sure to drape several around Sarah.

"Welcome, welcome, ladies!" The burlesque instructor—Georgina, I think—parades into the room with a tray of champagne glasses. "Is everyone ready to get their sexy on?"

"No," Sarah whimpers, at which everyone bursts out laughing.

The glasses of bubbly are passed around, and Georgina gets Sarah to share the story of how she and Aiden met, and then the proposal story. By the time Sarah's finished her champagne and her story-telling, she's standing behind her allocated chair, giggling and getting ready to learn her first burlesque moves.

Julia catches my eye and gives me a thumbs up. *Mission accomplished*, she mouths.

Despite the fact that I was secretly dreading the burlesque class almost as much as Sarah was, it turns out to be one of the most hilariously fun things I've done in ages. Certainly in the past year. Probably the past *two* years, if I'm honest with myself.

Everyone's still laughing and one or two of Sarah's friends are still practising their moves as we walk into Paolo's in Florida Road. Julia hired one of the small side rooms, so we steer Sarah past the dance floor and the tables and into the room decorated with pink and white streamers and other sparkly bits of decor. The cocktails Julia ordered beforehand are already waiting on the table at the centre of a large booth, along with a large glass jar filled with panties, and a—

"What is that?" Sarah exclaims, doubling over with laughter when she sees the board with four pairs of bras stuck to it, one above the other.

"That, my dear sister," Julia says, "is bra pong. See the numbers above each cup? That's how many points you get if you manage to get a ping pong ball into any of the cups."

"And the jar of panties?" Sarah asks between her giggles.

"Gifts. One pair from each of us. You have to guess who each pair of knickers is from."

"We had to buy you something that represents our personalities," Livi says, looping her arm through Sarah's and pulling her towards the table. "To help you guess."

"Personality panties," Sarah says with another chuckle. "I like it."

We all pile into the booth, grab a cocktail and a few ping pong balls, and Sarah starts trying to guess which panties come from whom. At some point after the panty game is done—and while ping pong balls fly randomly across the table at the bras—someone decides we should go around the table and give Sarah the worst possible marriage advice we can think of. That results in a whole lot more hilarity, and by the time I find myself in a one-on-one conversation with Livi as she interrogates me about my nonexistent love life, my stomach is aching from so much laughter.

"Come on!" Livi says, smacking me with a penis straw— which I will no doubt find highly disturbing when I think back on this moment later. "There's gotta be someone who occupies your thoughts. Someone your mind always turns to."

My thoughts go immediately to Lex, but that isn't something I can explain to her. And then, oddly enough, my next thought is Caleb. Probably because he's the only single guy I've spent any time with recently. I generally make a point of avoiding guys these days, but I haven't been able to do that with Caleb.

"There!" Livi says, pointing at my face, and I realise I'm smiling faintly. "Who are you thinking of right now?"

I do my best to get a blank expression in place as I roll my eyes. "I'm thinking of how peaceful my life will be once this wedding is over."

"Really?" She mimics my blank expression, then waves

the party pecker in my face.

I can't help the laughter that bursts out of my mouth.

Nobody keeps track of anyone's bra pong scores, so by the end of the evening, at least four girls are convinced they've won. Which doesn't really matter since it turns out there's no prize other than a sticker that says 'Bra Pong Champion,' which Livi decides to claim for herself and stick to her forehead, since she was the one who made it.

A little while later—and long after Mom and Dad have gone to bed, I'm sure—Sarah, Jules and I walk into the house with feather boas around our shoulders and party paraphernalia in our arms, still giggling as we recount the evening's most hilarious moments. We stagger into the lounge, drunk on laughter more than anything else, and find Josh, Aiden and Caleb still up.

"I guess we don't need to ask if you girls had fun," Aiden says, clicking the TV off and grinning at us.

"We *definitely* had fun," Julia tells them. We lower the bra pong, the jar of panties, and the box of ping pong balls onto the coffee table before the three of us collapse onto one couch.

"Whoa, hang on. What is that?" Josh asks. His words are followed by a hoot of laughter as he points to the bra pong board.

"Okay, whatever that game is," Caleb says, "I want to play."

"Here you go." I reach forward, grab a ping pong ball, and throw it at him. Then another and another. He scrambles to pick them up.

"Wait, wait, wait. Okay, I'm going first." He lines up his first shot while Josh and Aiden grab a few ping pong balls for themselves. They jostle for the best position.

Julia leans against Sarah and dissolves into more giggles. "I think they're having more fun with the bra pong than we did." She loops her arm through Sarah's and adds, "You enjoyed tonight, right? It wasn't too much, was it?"

"I loved it. I thought I might die of embarrassment when we walked into that burlesque class, but it turned out to be loads of fun."

"Do we get a demonstration?" Josh asks.

"Absolutely not," I tell him. "What happens in burlesque class stays in burlesque class."

"I'll give you a private demonstration later," Julia says, leaning past me to wink at her husband.

"Ew, gross." I push her back against the cushions. "Definitely too much information, Jules."

"Right, I think it's bed time then," Josh says, abandoning the bra pong and pulling Julia to her feet. He plants a quick kiss on her lips.

"Yep, bed time for me too," I announce, pushing myself up. "Before you guys start getting too affectionate." I wave goodnight over my shoulder and remove my shoes before heading down the passage. I'm still smiling as I climb the stairs to my room.

LuminaireX: Jeez. Is it appropriate for someone you just met to ask when last you cried in front of someone else? And what you think your biggest failure has been so far in life? And your most treasured memory?

AngelSH: Wow. First date?

LuminaireX: And last.

LuminaireX: I mean, I consider myself a pretty open person, but jeez. Give a guy a moment before you start the inquisition.

AngelSH: A moment? I would need at least five.

LuminaireX: Well, like I said … I'm the open one. I don't think we can say the same thing about you, Ash ;)

AngelSH: I'm pulling a rude gesture at you right now.

LuminaireX: Shocking! I'm positively horrified. (Also … I don't believe you ;-))

AngelSH: So when last did you cry in front of someone else?

LuminaireX: I thought we just decided that was an inappropriate question.

AngelSH: Only if you don't know me at all.

LuminaireX: Ummmmm … I don't know. It's been so long. Probably something to do with my parents.

LuminaireX: Oh yes. My dad came over to fetch me once for the weekend. We were supposed to go camping, just the two of us. He and my mother got into such a big fight right there on the doorstep that he ended up throwing a flower pot into the road and storming off. He didn't come back to see me for two months.

AngelSH: Hectic.

LuminaireX: Yeah. Parents suck sometimes.

AngelSH: Did you tell your date about that?

LuminaireX: Course not. My answer was: The other day, when I saw you for the first time. Your beauty was so overwhelming, I started crying.

AngelSH: .

AngelSH: .

AngelSH: That was the sound of me throwing up.

LuminaireX: Yeah, she didn't seem to believe me either ...

LuminaireX: When did you last cry in front of someone?

AngelSH: Um ... I think it's been about 4 months.

LuminaireX: That's quite specific. What happened 4 months ago?

AngelSH: I decided to stop crying.

LuminaireX: Well, yeah, but why?

AngelSH: Because crying is horrible.

LuminaireX: Buuuuut crying is always horrible. So what was different about 4 months ago?

AngelSH: Didn't we decide this was an inappropriate question?

LuminaireX: Nope. We didn't mention this exact question.

AngelSH: In that case, I've decided you don't know me well enough yet to ask this question.

LuminaireX: Well in THAT case, prepare for an onslaught of getting-to-know-you questions :D

LuminaireX: #1 - what's your favourite colour?

AngelSH: Oh, wow, is that the time? I have to go get my fingernails pulled out now. Chat later!

WEDNESDAY IS A SLOWER DAY. I GET UP EARLY TO CON-
tinue my various projects, but the house is quiet for much
longer than usual. After a late breakfast, Sarah and Aiden
sort out the seating chart for the reception—with many
unhelpful comments from Josh and Caleb—and I return to
my room so I don't have to be involved. I'd rather stab one
of my paintbrushes through my eyeball than decide where a
hundred and twenty people should sit for dinner.

I send a rough draft of the urban fantasy vampire
illustration to a client for suggestions, and do a little more
work on the steampunk poster draft. I answer a few query
emails, save two email confirmations of deposits that have
been paid, and schedule new projects into my calendar. I
also try to break my habit of checking my phone every half
hour for a message from Lex, which is the only part of my
day that I'm unsuccessful at.

In the early afternoon, Caleb reminds Aiden he hasn't seen much of Durban city centre yet, so Aiden and Josh quickly map out a DIY walking tour. Mom takes the opportunity to have an afternoon nap, but Sarah and Julia decide to join the guys. Relieved that I'll have the afternoon to myself, I announce I'll be staying home to finish a project or two.

Sarah catches me before I head back up to the attic and gives me a hug. "I wanted to say that it's nice to see you laughing so much and so easily. It's been far too long since I've seen you like this."

Despite the heat, I wrap my arms around myself. "Yeah, well, last night was fun. I don't think anyone could have gone through that without a tremendous amount of laughter."

They head out for their city tour, and I enjoy several hours of uninterrupted art time. They arrive home in the early evening, and about twenty minutes later we have to leave for our second—and last—dance class.

"Soph, can you explain this to me," Caleb says as half of us climb into Aiden's car and half into Sarah's. "Because nobody else seems to be able to." He twists around so he can look at me from the front passenger seat. "Bunny chow. It's a hollowed out loaf of bread with curry inside it, right? So where the heck does the name 'bunny chow' come from?"

I shrug. "Can't remember. So you had one today? At Victoria Street Market?"

"I did."

"And did you like it?"

"I'm not sure. I can't feel my tongue yet."

"A little too hot for you?" I ask with a chuckle.

"Just a little."

Nick and Livi are already practising when we walk into the school hall. "Are we late?" Sarah asks, hurrying inside.

"No, no. Just in time," Lucille says, sashaying towards us. "We will practise without music to start, just to make sure you remember everything. Sarah and Aiden, you practise the new steps from last time. The rest of you, your steps are simple. Come, come." She snaps her fingers repeatedly. "Don't waste time. You don't want to embarrass your bride and groom on the wedding day."

I'm still of the opinion that these dance lessons are a silly idea, but in keeping with my commitment to make Sarah happy, I move quickly to stand in front of Caleb and raise my arms. With my left hand on his shoulder and my right hand in his grasp, we start our somewhat stilted walk, walk, side, tap to an imaginary beat.

"I hope you've been warming up your dance shoes for Saturday night, Miss Henley," Caleb says, "in preparation for all the dancing we'll be doing together."

I move my gaze from the hall stage to Caleb's face. "Why would I do such a thing when you have no hope of winning the bet?"

His eyes crinkle at the edges. "I think I'm a whole lot closer to winning the bet than I was during our last dance class."

"Well, I think you're wrong." He probably isn't wrong,

but I don't want to admit that yet.

"I saw how much fun you had last night."

"Perhaps, but that wasn't the wedding."

"It was wedding related."

"I'm pretty sure that doesn't count."

"If it moves you closer towards having fun on Saturday night," he says, "then it does."

"Okay," Lucille says loudly. "You know the steps, but you don't look very natural."

"Not sure it's possible to look natural after only two lessons," I whisper to Caleb.

"I think the music will help," Lucille continues. "Sarah and Aiden, in the middle of the dance floor please. The rest of you stand to the side. You remember when to join in, yes?" She raises her heavily penciled eyebrows as she surveys us. We nod.

Lucille signals to her young assistant standing on the other side of the hall, and the music begins. We watch Sarah and Aiden as they walk, walk, side, tap, looking better than they did last week. When Aiden dips Sarah down, that's our cue to walk onto the dance floor. As he pulls her up and continues dancing, we join in. Caleb and I begin moving a little late, but we soon manage to settle into the beat.

"This is a lot more enjoyable than our first lesson," he comments.

"I guess."

"At least you don't hate me anymore."

"Look, I never actually *hated* you. I just found you—"

A song starts playing over the tinny sound of the music

we're dancing to. "Oops, my bad." Caleb stops and reaches for his front jeans pocket. "Shoulda put that on silent." He raises his phone and looks at the screen—and hesitates. "Um, I should probably take this." He steps away from me and heads for the hall door, raising the phone to his ear as he goes.

Lucille, looking unimpressed, tells me to continue practising on my own—as if that isn't super awkward. I start a shuffle version of the steps, slowly edging towards the hall door as I go. Through the glass upper half of the door, I can see Caleb. He walks back and forth across the foyer, pushing one hand through his short hair and tugging at it. I shuffle around some more, not wanting to incur Lucille's wrath, occasionally looking through the door to check that Caleb's still there.

When he eventually returns to the hall, there's no trace of his ever-present smile. "Sorry about that," he says. "Shall we carry on?"

But the music stops at that moment. Lucille shouts a few instructions, and Sarah and Aiden start from the beginning of their dance again. From the corner of my eye, I take a peek at Caleb.

"What?" he asks when he notices me watching him.

"Uh, it's just … I think this is the first time since we've met that you've looked less than happy."

He nods slowly. "That's probably true."

"I thought you had this annoyingly easy ability to be happy all the time."

"Huh, I wish. I mean, a lot of the time it is easy, but

sometimes …" He lets out a long sigh. "Sometimes it isn't. Sometimes happiness is a choice, and I have to make the effort to choose it." He gives me a smile, but it's a poor imitation of his normal beaming grin.

"Like right now?"

"I guess." He nudges my arm with his elbow and turns to watch the bridal couple. "But give me a few minutes and it won't be an effort anymore. Unhappy spells never last long."

Maybe for you, I think to myself. In my experience, 'unhappy spells' are hard to shake.

"Come, come, come," Lucille shouts, snapping her fingers. "You are missing your cue."

I jump into action as I realise the others are already moving to join Sarah and Aiden. Caleb and I fumble with hands and arms and getting into position, but we're just in time to join in at the right moment. Sarah frowns at me over Aiden's shoulder. I mouth, *Sorry!* I'll have to tell her later that our delay was due to me being *nice* to Caleb, not arguing with him.

We dance in silence for a while, which feels odd now that I've become used to Caleb's continual chatter. Our roles are reversed with him staring past me while I keep sneaking looks at his face. I should be happy to let us continue in silence—after all, I'm the one who's no longer interested in interaction with people who aren't family members or existing friends—but the silence is so abnormal that I feel I have to fill it.

"Can I ask who was on the phone?"

"Uh, yeah." Caleb blinks and focuses his gaze on me. "It

146

was my mom. She's, uh, thinking about divorcing Husband Number Three."

"Oh, wow." That was a whole lot more than I was expecting. "I'm … sorry?" Without knowing a single thing about Caleb's mom or her third husband, I don't know if this divorce would be a good thing or not.

"I told her I'm not interested in hearing about this one. If she can't make any of her marriages work, it isn't my problem."

My next questions are tentative. "What about your dad? Is he also remarried?"

"He's with Wife Number Two, but they have issues as well. Don't know how long that one will last."

"I'm sorry. Divorce really sucks."

"Yeah." Caleb looks over my shoulder again. "It could have been worse, though. There was this old lady who lived next door. She had a library of kids' books for whenever her grandchildren visited, so I used to go over and borrow them. When my parents were fighting—before the divorce—I would just stay at Mrs Taylor's house for hours and read. If it was a Sunday, she'd take me to church with her."

"Oh, you poor thing."

"No, I actually liked it," Caleb says with a chuckle. "Everyone was friendly, and Sunday school was fun, and when I asked people why life sucked so much, they took the time to give me decent answers."

"Like what?"

"Like … 'You think life sucks for you? Look at what

Jesus went through.'"

I shake my head at that, but I can't help laughing along with Caleb. "Does that really make any difference to a kid? Pointing out that life isn't so bad because at least you didn't get beaten up by a crazed mob and then nailed to two pieces of wood and left to die?"

"Well, maybe that part didn't help," he admits, "but when someone reminded me of the street kids who had no home and no food, that stuck with me. I told my mom about it, and she used it to point out that God clearly doesn't care about anyone. But then ... I noticed that she didn't do anything about it, while all the old grannies at church got together every week and made sandwiches for one of the shelters. So ..." Caleb shrugs. "I decided to ignore my mom and stick with what the grannies said."

I nod. "I guess sometimes the old ladies know best."

"Yep. I kept trying to get my mom to go with me, but she wasn't interested. I tried with Aiden too, since he was my best friend and I figured Sunday school would be more fun with him there, but he wasn't interested either. Only changed his mind after meeting Sarah."

I continue nodding slowly, wondering where to direct the conversation next. Wondering why I even care. "Um ..." I take a deep breath. "You know I didn't actually hate you when we met, right? I'm just ... very ..." I search for a word that doesn't sound negative. Not *bitchy*, not *rude*, not *stand-offish*. "Guarded. I'm very guarded."

"I know," he says. "Sophie ..." Slowly, perhaps without even realising it, he stops dancing. Which means, of course, that I stop dancing too.

"Yes?" I feel my eyebrows tug together in confusion.

"Um … never mind."

"Seriously? You're going to look at me with such concern and then tell me to 'never mind'?"

"What happened?" he asks, which doesn't clear up my confusion in the slightest.

"What happened with what?" I ask.

"You two!" Lucille shouts, her snapping fingers suddenly right beside my ear. "Never paying attention."

I step back, realising suddenly that the music has stopped and everyone in the room is looking at us.

"Oops," Caleb says.

"We are starting from the beginning again," Lucille tells us, "so you need to move away."

I hurry to the edge of the room, Caleb close behind me. His hand brushes my elbow as he leans closer and whispers, "Why do I feel like we're always the naughty ones in this class?"

"I think we are the naughty ones," I say with a light laugh.

Sarah catches my eye and gives me a curious look. I know what she's thinking, so I give her a quick shake of my head. But there's a sensation in the region of my stomach that I recognise. A faint lurch I haven't felt since … since I first noticed Braden. I dismiss the feeling immediately. In fact, I almost want to laugh at it. What business do my insides have getting swoony over a guy I barely know who'll be leaving in a few days? Absolutely none, that's what. My emotions are all mixed up with the relief of finally finishing school, the joy of being able to devote all my free time to my art, and all the overflowing wedding excitement that keeps rubbing off on me. This flutter in my stomach has nothing to do with Caleb and his ever-present smile and contagious laugh. I most certainly won't be breaking my rule for him.

I do want to know what he was talking about on the dance floor, though, but he's speaking with Josh now. They're pointing at Aiden as he and Sarah begin their dance again, snickering at something. *Boys*, I think to myself with an internal sigh. Some of them never seem to grow up.

By the time it's our turn to join the dance floor again, Caleb's mood has shifted back to the one I'm familiar with. He chats away about nonsense, never giving me a chance to ask him what he was talking about just now.

"And that's all we have time for," Lucille calls as the music ends for the last time. "You have the hang of it now, and you will all look lovely on Saturday. But maybe practise once more in private." She eyes Caleb and me as she says this. "Aiden, Sarah—" she kisses each of them on the cheek "—I wish you many years of happiness together."

After thanking Lucille, we all head out to the parking lot together. Sarah, Julia and Livi chat about jewellery for Saturday, and the guys laugh about something they saw while walking the streets of Durban this afternoon.

The next thing I know, Caleb is tugging a dark hood over Aiden's head and shoving him into the backseat of his own car. Sarah gasps and claps a hand over her mouth. "Bachelor party time!" Josh shouts, running around the car and jumping into the driver's seat.

"Oh my goodness, please don't hurt him," Sarah mumbles.

Julia laughs and wraps an arm around Sarah's shoulders. "He'll be totally fine."

LuminaireX: Hey, we should collaborate on some stuff. We can call ourselves ... Ashlex.

AngelSH: That username's probably taken already.

LuminaireX: Ever the optimist.

AngelSH: That's me :)

LuminaireX: What would we paint together?

AngelSH: I don't know. This was your idea.

LuminaireX: We probably wouldn't be able to agree on a subject.

AngelSH: Probably.

LuminaireX: Which could make for a very interesting end product, actually.

AngelSH: Maybe I don't want you messing with my end product.

LuminaireX: Fine. But you're totally missing out by not getting involved with this creative genius ;)

AngelSH: Ha! Creative genius, my butt.

LuminaireX: Your butt is a creative genius?

AngelSH: It is. And my creative genius butt is going to bed now because it's tired of the nonsense coming out of your non-creative genius butt.

LuminaireX: This is probably one of the strangest conversations I've ever had.

AngelSH: Yeah. Me too. Night, Lex.

LuminaireX: Night, Ash.

16

I WAKE UP AROUND ONE IN THE MORNING AND CAN'T GO back to sleep. After kicking my duvet off and downing the glass of water beside my bed, I'm still too hot and uncomfortable to fall asleep. I sit up, rub my eyes, and turn my lamp on. May as well get something done instead of lying here uselessly.

I'm too tired to sit at my desk and do any actual drawing, so I remain in bed and reach for my iPad. I search my favourite online spots for inspiration, saving everything I like to various private Pinterest boards and typing a few notes in case I've forgotten my brilliant moments of inspiration when I wake up in the morning.

My iPad says 1:47 a.m. when I hear the squeak and creak of the gate opening. My first reaction is panic—Who the hell is opening our gate in the middle of the night?—but then I remember the guys had Aiden's bachelor party tonight. Of course they're only coming home now. But I get out of bed and pull my curtain aside to check anyway. Yep, that's Aiden's car.

I climb back into bed. I reach for my water, then remember I finished it. I look through another gallery on DeviantArt, giving the guys enough time to get to their beds downstairs. Then I climb out of bed, take my empty glass, and head to the kitchen for some iced water. I assume everyone's fast asleep by now, but when I walk into the lounge, I find someone sitting in the semi-darkness on one of the couches. It's Caleb, his face lit up by the light of his cell phone.

"Oh," I say. "Why are you still awake?"

"Why are *you* still awake?" he asks as he looks up.

I shrug. "Not sure really. Too hot, I think. I just can't get comfortable."

"Yeah, the heat is something else here. I expected it, obviously, but that doesn't really help when you're in the midst of it."

"Nope. I'm just getting some water." I gesture towards the kitchen, in case he had any doubt as to where I plan to get this water from. *Idiot, Sophie.* "Uh, would you like some?"

"Yes, thanks. I was on my way to get a glass and ended up distracted along the way." His gaze returns to his phone. He begins tapping away at the screen as I head for the kitchen.

"How was the bachelor party?" I ask when I return with a glass of water in each hand. I set them both down on the coffee table and sit in one of the single armchairs.

"I think everyone had fun. It was quite tame, I guess. No strippers, if that's what you were wondering."

I chuckle quietly. "Look, I'm not entirely sure about you, but I know Josh well enough to be fairly certain he would never get strippers involved. Aiden would be super uncomfortable with that."

"And Sarah would kill us," Caleb adds.

"Yes. I guess things didn't get too raucous if you're home so early."

"Or maybe we're just getting too old for this kinda thing."

I smile, reach for my glass, and lean back against the cushions. "I half expected you guys to stumble in here totally wasted at like five in the morning and then pass out on the floor halfway down the passage."

Caleb raises an eyebrow. "You just told me you know Josh well."

"I do."

"And I assume you know Aiden pretty well too."

"Yep."

"Then you know that winding up horrendously drunk was never an option for tonight."

"Yeah, I guess." I tap my fingernail against the side of the glass. "But you never know what might happen when there are other guys around. Guys who think excessive drinking is compulsory." I make a show of sniffing the air. "But you don't smell too bad. Only a hint of alcohol and cigarette smoke."

"Thanks," he says, amusement sparkling in his eyes. His

phone screen lights up for a moment. He looks down, his smile slipping away. But instead of replying to whatever he sees there, he turns the phone over.

"What distracted you just now when you came to get water?" I ask.

He takes in a long, slow breath before answering. "An email from my mom. Apparently I ended our phone call too soon earlier, and she had more to tell me. Or more to try and explain, I guess." He leans back with a sigh and stares at the ceiling. "I'm so scared I might end up like them, you know?"

I pause with my lips parted, unsure of how to respond. I don't do this kind of thing anymore, getting personal with people. It's so much easier to maintain a safe distance when nothing serious is ever discussed. But I can't respond to Caleb admitting his fear by simply getting up and leaving. Even I'm not that cruel. "Like … end up divorced?"

"Yes. I mean, how can you predict something like that? Nobody goes into a marriage planning for it to fail, so how can you ever know if you've chosen the right person? My mother's got it wrong three times, and my dad got it wrong at least once, possibly twice. What if I end up just like them?"

He's asking me, the person who's sworn off love forever, for an answer about choosing the right person? "Honestly … I don't know." My mind flashes to Lex for a moment. Could he possibly have been the right person for me if we'd met in real life instead of online? No, I doubt it. He's probably a completely different person in real life. Like me, he's probably kept all the dark parts of his life hidden, and I wouldn't judge him for a second if he did. "I'm sorry, Caleb," I say quietly, "but I'm not the person to answer that question. You're trying to figure out how to choose the right person, but I've decided the right person doesn't exist for me. You want to have a marriage one day that lasts, whereas I don't want one at all. So, I … I don't know."

He tilts his head to the side and gives me a sleepy half-smile. "What if it were you?"

"Um … you mean, what if I were the one with the divorced parents?"

He looks up at the ceiling again and closes his eyes. I think he murmurs something else, but it's too quiet for me to hear. Watching him, I remember this isn't the first time he's confused me with a question this evening. Earlier, he wanted to know 'what happened,' and he still hasn't explained that. "Um … Caleb?" He doesn't answer. "Caleb," I repeat quietly. His steady breathing is the only response.

I chew on my lip for several moments, wondering if I should wake him and send him to a real bed. I've slept on this couch before, and it isn't particularly comfortable. Especially not the way he's sleeping on it, upright with his head tilted back. I take a sip of water, then stand and walk to his side. "Caleb." I touch his arm, giving it a light squeeze, but all he does is mumble, slide down, and turn over.

Well. I guess that'll have to be good enough for him. Reminding myself that it's totally creepy to stare for too long, I turn and head back upstairs.

"Is this the correct length of the aisle?" Tim asks on Thursday afternoon as the bridal party crowds into my parents' lounge.

"Yes, I measured it more than once," Sarah says. She fans her face with her hand, as if that could possibly combat the heat any better than the three fans that are already positioned around the lounge.

"Okay. I'll be up at the front, obviously," Tim says as he walks to the other end of the room, which is currently doubling as the front of the church. "And the guys will be with me." Aiden and his groomsmen join Tim, taking a few moments to arrange themselves in whatever order they've decided on. On our end of the room, Sarah steers us into a line with Livi at the front, then me, then Julia. "And I'm at the back, obviously," she mutters to herself.

The thought of just how silly this whole process is

crosses my mind once again. But every hairy eyeball in the room will turn on me if I voice that thought out loud, so I simply wait patiently in line and keep my mouth shut.

"And you've got your music?" Tim asks.

"Yes, got it right here," Sarah answers, waving her phone.

"All right. Start the music, and we'll see how it goes."

"Okay, so I'm thinking you should walk about halfway," Sarah tells us, "and then the next person starts."

We nod. Sarah hurries to the back of our line, and slow, old-fashioned music begins playing from her cell phone. It wouldn't be my first choice. Then again, I don't plan to ever go through something like this, so I never have to decide what music would work for me.

"Not so quickly," Sarah says to Livi.

"Seriously? I feel like I'm almost walking backwards I'm going so slowly," Livi says as she moves down the makeshift aisle towards Tim and the guys.

"It always feels slower than it actually is," Tim says with a chuckle.

"Start walking now, Soph," Julia says, prodding me forward.

"Okay, okay," I mutter. I didn't think Livi was halfway yet, but whatever. I'm not in charge here.

"Maybe we should rather have an exact moment in the music when we each begin walking," Julia suggests. "Like we did at my wedding."

"*Our* wedding," Josh says, then winks at her.

"I don't think that would work with this piece of music," Sarah says. "It sounds kind of the same the whole way, just building in intensity."

"If we know the number of pews at the church," Julia says, "then we can decide on exactly which pew each bridesmaid should reach before the next one starts walking."

I close my eyes for a moment, breathing out the words "Oh my goodness" on a sigh. "Do we really have to be so precise?"

"Let's just get everyone to the front now and run through the order of service," Tim says as I take another painfully slow step forward. "Then you ladies can adjust your timing as much as you want. And I think you might be going a little *too* slowly, Soph," he adds with a smile.

"Would you like to walk next to me and demonstrate, Tim?"

Tim laughs. "Perhaps I should. I never got the chance to be the one to walk down the aisle." When we're finally all standing in a line in front of him, he adds, "Oh, and parents? We need you up here as well. If you could stand roughly where you'll be sitting on Saturday, that would be great."

The chatter from the side of the room stops as my parents and Aiden's mom hurry to join us. Aidan's mother arrived this morning, along with Aiden's sister and brother-in-law, Emily and Harry. They've been hanging out here for most of the afternoon, getting ready for our giant family dinner this evening.

"Okay, are we ready to run through everything?" Tim asks.

"This is so weird," Sarah whispers. "Remember when we

were all kids, and you were one of the youth leaders, and now you're *marrying* us."

He nods and smiles. "Yep. Now we're all grown-up."

After Tim has run through the entire order of service with us, and everyone knows at what point they're sitting, standing, exchanging rings, lighting candles and all the rest of it, we have to walk down our pretend aisle FIVE MORE TIMES. Five times until Sarah is happy that everyone will be walking into the chapel at the right time and the right speed.

And when we're finally done and I'm hoping to go lie on my bed with my phone for an hour or so to chat with Lex, Mom announces that we have twenty-five minutes until we need to leave for dinner.

I drag myself upstairs—it's too hot for anything that might resemble running—and change out of my shorts and tank top. Scrunch yawns, turns in a circle, and repositions himself on my bed. "Lucky you," I say to him. "You don't have to go out and be happy and chatty." Although the happy part isn't so difficult for me anymore, as Sarah pointed out yesterday. Probably because the wedding is almost upon us, and I'll soon have all the time in the world to do my own thing. "Won't that be wonderful?" I say to Scrunch, who half-opens one eye before licking his lips and continuing to ignore me.

I turn to my cupboard. I remove the first summer dress I find and pull it over my head. But when I look at myself in the mirror stuck to the inside of the cupboard door, I wonder if perhaps I should search my clothes for something prettier. This is a special occasion, as everyone keeps reminding everyone else, so I should probably make more of an effort. I pull the dress off—breaking out in a sweat from the exertion—and find a dress with a prettier pattern and a more flattering shape. *There*, I think to myself as I swivel and examine my appearance. *Doesn't hurt to look nice.*

Wait. It doesn't hurt to *look nice*? I shake my head at my reflection and whisper, "That is the stupidest thought you've had in a long time. Who the heck are you trying to look nice for?"

My reflection and I are both aware of the answer, so I simply bang the cupboard door shut and look around the room for some appropriate shoes. Cream pumps stick out from beneath my desk, so I slip my feet into them. After waiting for my two minutes in the bathroom, I spritz on some body spray, dab on some lip gloss, and drag a mascara wand over my lashes. Anything more than that will probably melt off my face before we reach the restaurant, so there's no point in wasting time with it.

I squish into the back of a car with Emily and Harry. Mom and Dad sit in the front where they get to experience most of the cool air flying out of the car's air vents. Here in the back seat, perspiration sticks my dress to me.

The breeze is warm when we climb out of the car in one of the parking lots alongside Durban's beachfront, but I appreciate the fact that the air is at least moving. The other two cars left home after us, so we begin a slow stroll along the promenade, reaching the restaurant Mom booked for a us a few minutes later. Situated right on the beachfront with a great view of the sea, the restaurant has pushed several tables together to accommodate our large group. Part of me wonders what the point of this dinner is. Won't we be doing this all over again in two nights time, just with smarter clothes, more expensive food, and a few more people?

Mom is busy pointing out where she thinks everyone should sit when the rest of our group arrives. "Hey, you look nice," Caleb says to me, the words rolling easily off his tongue, as if he throws compliments out to women all the time. Feeling that lurch in my stomach once more, part of me wants to distance myself immediately. But he's here for only another few days, and Sarah wants me to be polite, so I may as well enjoy his company while he's around. Laugh, let myself smile, indulge in a few stomach-fluttering moments. Possibly even lose the bet I made with him. Then he'll be gone, and perhaps I'll feel down for a day or two, but I'll be safe. And I'll still have Lex. Everything will return to normal.

So when it looks like Caleb's going to end up sitting across the table from me, I let it happen instead of moving further along. Two waiters bustle about, handing out menus and asking if anyone wants to order a drink so long.

Once we're all settled, Caleb leans forward and says, "Hey, did I fall asleep in the middle of a conversation about my parents last night? I can't quite remember, but I know I woke up on a couch I hadn't planned to fall asleep on."

"Well, sort of, but we weren't really saying much at the time. It would have been funny if you'd fallen asleep mid-sentence, though."

He laughs. "That's kind of how it felt."

"I was just worried you were going to end up having an awful night on that couch. It isn't the most comfortable thing to sleep on."

"It wasn't too bad." He opens the menu in front of him and scans the first page. "What's good to eat here?"

"I don't know. I think I've only been here once before, and I don't remember what I ate." It was a dinner with Braden and his parents. Not one of my happiest memories.

We discuss the menu—arguing about which is better between a seafood platter and a sushi platter—until the two waiters return to take everyone's order. When they're done, I look through my handbag for a pen and some form of scrap paper. I find a slightly crumpled flier from Mary's Arts & Crafts which is blank on one side. As I begin sketching, I ask Caleb what he has planned for the rest of his South Africa holiday other than visiting a game reserve. He lists the Drakensberg and a whole bunch of places around Cape Town, and when he's done, I push the paper and pen across the table to him. "Your turn."

We chat a little more about his mom as he moves the pen back and forth in short strokes across the page. She hasn't contacted him again since last night, but now a nosey friend of hers has sent Caleb a message saying that his mother is ignoring her after an argument the two of them had, and can he please intervene.

"I said no," he tells me as he passes the paper and pen back to me.

"Good. That doesn't sound like something you need to get involved in." I look down at the page. Caleb has added a little boy sitting on top of my monster tree, and the headless horse I drew galloping across the sky is now a polka-dot headless horse. I add a few more details—clouds filled with stars—and send the drawing back across the table.

"Do you hear from your dad often?" I ask him.

"Not much. Not nearly as much as my mom. She's always telling me about her problems, whereas my dad seems to want to hide his from me. Anyway, this conversation is quickly becoming depressing, so let's change the subject."

"Okay. Um …"

"How's your steampunk poster coming along?"

I lean back and take a sip of iced water before answering. "I think it's going to be really cool when it's done, but I also think it's going to take me longer than I thought."

"Is that a problem for the client?"

"No. I told her I may need more time, and she was fine with that. She liked the draft I sent her, so that's good."

"Cool," Caleb says. "Aaaaand there." He makes one last flourish in the bottom corner before smacking the pen down onto the page and pushing both back towards me. "Done."

I look at his additions to the drawing. "A poodle's head?" I say through my laughter. "On top of my headless horse? That is *not* what I was going for. At all. And what is that thing on its tail?"

"It's a string. Because the horse-poodle is actually a balloon, and the boy sitting in the tree is holding the other end of the string."

I lean back in my chair, shaking my head but still smiling as I examine the rest of the ridiculous finishing touches Caleb has added. And then … all the blood rushes from my body in one go. Because the signature, the scrawl in the lower right corner, the loop-scribble-loop …

Loop-scribble-loop.

The evening remains oppressively hot, but goosebumps raise the hairs across my arms. My smile freezes. Falters. Vanishes.

"What's wrong?" Caleb asks.

It can't be. It can't be it can't be it can't be.

Slowly, I raise my eyes from the page and look at him. At his happy, freckled, entirely non-Asian face. My world tilts, adjusts, realigns, and somewhere along the way, Caleb's confused smile disappears. He knows. He knows what he's done, and he knows that I know, and he knows who I am and HOW THE ACTUAL HELL?

Caleb sucks in a breath, preparing to say something, but then he slowly deflates. His shoulders droop, and his breath leaves him in a single word: "Bollocks."

"Caleb!" Mom says, whipping her head around as her swear-word detector goes off.

Caleb replies, but I'm not sure what he says because I'm already standing. Then I'm walking, angling my body between the tables and chairs, and leaving the restaurant.

No way. No. Way. I know the world is small, but it isn't *that* small. There's no way that my Internet crush is also my sister's fiancé's best man. There's just no flipping way!

My feet carry me along the promenade and onto one of the piers. Eventually I stop walking and lean on the railing. I stare down at the churning water below. My brain keeps rejecting the idea, and yet it must be true. Caleb's face said as much. And he already *knew*! How the hell did he know that I'm—

My art. He saw my paintings and sketches stuck all over my walls. Prints of digital work that I've uploaded to Artster over the years. That's why he looked so stunned the first time he walked into my room.

I bury my face in my hands and groan. This is so damn confusing and so *embarrassing*. Lex knows far too much about me. More than anyone in real life ever should, which means Caleb knows all those things too. And why didn't he *say* anything? Why did he go on pretending he didn't know me at all?

"How did this happen?" I murmur between my fingers. I don't even remember how I first discovered his work. Is it simply a gigantic coincidence that he's connected to me in real life?

I step back from the railing, take a seat on the nearest bench, and remove my phone from my handbag. I open the email app and tap on the search bar at the top. I get notifications from just about every social media platform I'm signed up to, and I never delete anything, so there must be a record of our first interaction. I type 'Luminaire' into the search bar. A bazillion results show up, and I start scrolling down. Down, down, down, back through time to the earliest emails from about two years ago. Facebook, Facebook, Facebook … Yes, that's right. I found his Facebook page first. But I don't think I knew Aiden back then, so this must be the world's biggest co—

But then I reach the final page and see the very first email: a notification of a Facebook message from Sarah.

Found this cool artist's page on FB. The Luminaire Artist. Kinda reminds me of some of your stuff. Check it out.

Ho-ly crap. It was never a coincidence.

I lower my phone into my lap and stare, unseeingly, out at the water. Lex and I have been connected all along and I never realised it. Perhaps because I hardly ever use Facebook anymore. Once I discovered art-focused social media platforms, I stuck to those instead, and my family doesn't use any of them, so there was no one else to make the connection between Lex and me. I lean forward, rest my elbows on my knees, and press my fingers to my temples.

Why am I so upset? I shouldn't be upset. Lex and Caleb are the same person, but so what? It shouldn't freak me out so completely. This isn't a big deal.

But it is, my panicked self reminds me. This thing with Lex … it was safe. It was contained. It was on my cell phone and my iPad and my computer and *that was it*. Real life could never touch or taint it. But now …

My phone buzzes against my lap. I open my eyes and look down. It's an Artster notification informing me of a message from LuminaireX—of course. I shake my head but swipe my thumb across the phone's surface to open the app anyway. What else would I do? Ignore a message from Lex? I don't think I'm capable of that.

LuminaireX: I get it. I should have said something the first time I came into your room and realised who you are. But COME ON. You were looking at me like you'd never hated anyone so much. I didn't want to ruin our online friendship for the sake of a little honesty.

LuminaireX: Okay, that sounded terrible. Obviously honesty is important. I value honesty. And I did plan to tell you at some point. Some point AFTER you realised that I'm not the worst person in the world and that you actually like me in real life too, not just online. Like now.

LuminaireX: Right? You don't hate me anymore in real life, do you?

LuminaireX: I mean, obviously right at this moment you do, but in general … overall … not counting this moment … you don't hate me, right?

Still holding the phone, I cover my face once more and release another groan. Of course I don't hate him. He's *Lex*, and I could never hate Lex. And Caleb … I like him too. I like dancing with him and drawing with him and laughing with him. Laughing—what a novel concept. I think I've laughed more in the past few days than I have in all the other days of this year combined. So it definitely isn't hatred that I'm feeling. Nope, I'm pretty sure it's something approaching complete mortification. Just thinking back on all the messages I've sent Lex, a person I never planned to look in the eye in real life, makes me cringe. All those private, secret things. And now he's a *real person* in my *real life*!

I slump back against the bench and lock my phone's screen without replying.

Lex is Caleb.

Caleb is Lex.

The more I think about it, the more stupid I feel. Of *course* they're the same person. They speak the same way. They're both skilled artists. They're both so irritatingly positive.

"Sophie."

Lost as I am in my thoughts, the sound of my name makes me flinch. I look up and find him standing there, his arms hanging awkwardly at his sides. "Can I sit here?" he asks.

And though I'm far from ready for this, I breathe out slowly and nod.

"ANGELSH," CALEB SAYS QUIETLY AFTER WE'VE SAT IN silence for at least a full minute. "S and H for Sophie Henley, and angel because ... you always got stuck playing an angel in nativity plays?"

I sense him turning his head to look at me, but I keep my gaze pointed firmly ahead. I wish I could pull my knees up and hug them, but unfortunately I'm wearing a dress.

"You're ... not quite what I imagined," he says when I don't respond.

"Sorry to disappoint you," I murmur, still staring forward.

"That isn't—" He stops himself and shifts to face me. "You know that isn't what I meant. It's just ... you sounded a little older, that's all. Or maybe I'm completely immature, so that's why I was imagining you the same age as—"

"Why didn't you say anything?" I snap, turning to him

173

suddenly. "You've known for days, and yet you left me in complete ignorance. Do you have any idea how embarrassing this is?"

"Embarrassing? Why would—"

"Because you know *everything about me*!"

He shakes his head. "Not everything. In fact, if anyone should be embarrassed in this situation, it's me. I've definitely shared more over the past two years than you have."

I let out a huff of breath and face the waves again. As if Caleb could ever be embarrassed about anything. "Why … why did you think I was older? You knew about my exams. It doesn't take a genius to figure out that exams mean school."

"You only ever mentioned the art exams. I thought they were for university or college or something. And who says older people can't take exams?"

I bite my lip and cross one leg over the other. I'm still itching to pull my knees up, and still afraid that I'll end up flashing my underwear to whoever happens to walk past. "Well … I thought you were a skinny Asian guy."

He laughs, loudly and unabashedly. "Because of my profile picture."

I fix him with a frown. He shouldn't be laughing at this. At us. Eventually he seems to get the hint. "Sophie," he says slowly, seriously. "Ash … AngelSH … I like you. I like our online interaction. I thought you might never send me another message ever again if you found out that Aiden's rude best friend, the guy you were so determined not to like, was also the guy you chatted to online every day. And, you know, you made it pretty clear the other day that you didn't want to meet me—LuminaireX—in real life. So there was that too … But I promise I wasn't trying to embarrass you."

I nod slowly. "It's not that I didn't *want* to meet you. I just thought … it would be less complicated if I didn't."

"Why?"

Because you mean too much to me already and it might hurt more than I can handle when we have to say goodbye.

Right. Like I'm really going to say that out loud. So I say nothing instead.

"Okay then," Caleb says. "So … where do we stand now?"

"I don't know. This just feels really weird."

"Weird in a good way, right?"

"Just … weird." I look at him again, really look at him, and try to think of him as Lex. "You—Caleb—don't really seem like the kind of guy to hang out online all the time. It sounds like you have plenty of friends in real life. What do you need Internet friends for?"

"One can never have too many friends, right?"

I raise an eyebrow.

"Okay, clearly you don't feel the same way, but I'm always happy to make more friends." He slides a bit closer, making the gap between us even smaller. Oddly enough, I find myself okay with that. "Look, not everyone in real life understands the kind of art you and I do," Caleb says. "I mean, how do people usually react when you tell them you draw pictures of fantasy creatures and settings?"

"I don't usually tell people that."

"Exactly. Because most people think it's a bit strange. Sure, I've met some other artists who do the same sort of thing, but there's a much larger community of them online. So when I feel like talking about that kinda thing, that's where I hang out."

I stare at my clasped hands in my lap and switch the way my legs are crossed. "Okay."

"Anything else you want me to explain to help make this less weird?" he asks.

"I'm trying to meld the two of you together in my mind, but it's difficult. You're the same, but not the same. Talking to you is almost exactly like talking to LuminaireX. But then … you're also different. I mean, you come across as kind of a player."

His eyes widen at that. "Excuse me?"

"No, sorry, I didn't mean to be rude. I'm—" I roll my eyes and sigh. "You know I've been trying hard to put my rude comments aside. I just mean that you've had, like, a zillion girlfriends in the past few years. Apparently there've been so many that Jules can't keep up with them all."

Caleb shakes his head, a small smile reappearing. "It isn't like that."

My eyes scan his face, searching for any hint of deception. "What's it like then?"

"I'm still looking for the right person. I'm not a casual fling kinda guy, so if I know it isn't going to work out long-term with someone, then I don't see the point in continuing a romantic relationship. Friendship, yes. I'm happy to be friends with everyone. But more than that … well, I'm still searching."

I shift to face him and pull one leg up beneath me. It feels less formal, while still keeping me from flashing my undies at anyone. "So, you're what? On this great quest to find a wife?"

He scratches his head. "Sounds kinda weird when you put it that way. More like … dating with purpose."

"That sounds just as weird."

He shrugs. "Then label me weird."

"Weirdo," I mutter, but I'm almost smiling now. This feels a little bit like an out-loud version of texting with Lex. "Maybe you haven't given any of these girls enough of a chance. Sounds like you move on from each of them pretty quickly. How can you know if they're right or wrong for you in so short a time?"

"I guess because I know what I'm looking for, and I didn't find it in any of those girls."

"Maybe you didn't look hard enough."

"I shouldn't have to *look hard*," he says with a laugh. "It should just be there. You either click or you don't click."

"And what's this magic 'click' element you're looking for?"

"It's …" He leans away from me and scratches the back of his neck, looking uncomfortable. His gaze turns towards the sea. "I guess I can't really explain it."

I hesitate, remembering what we spoke about late last night—or early this morning—and suddenly his persistent search for the 'right person' makes sense. "You don't want to end up like your parents."

He looks at me again, his gaze more intense than usual. "No. I don't."

"But how can you ever know for sure if you've found the right person?"

He chews his lip, perhaps considering his answer. "I think I'll just know."

Aaaaand that doesn't sound like a particularly solid answer.

Caleb clears his throat and rolls his shoulders a few times. "Since we're getting everything out in the open now, I have a confession."

"Oh dear."

"It isn't anything *bad*," he assures me. "It's just that after you disappeared from Artster and all the other sites, I tried to find you. Like, I tried to find the real person behind AngelSH. Not in a stalker way, but just … I was worried about you. I wanted to check you were okay. Anyway, I couldn't find you."

"Yeah, I tend to keep my personal stuff completely separate from my art stuff online."

"Well, at least you came back. I spent several months *wracked* with debilitating concern, wondering if my dark art had forever scarred you and sent you into hiding."

I roll my eyes and push him away. "Your dark art? You mean that unicorn puke you painted the other day?"

"Hey, I was travelling to the Rainbow Nation. I felt like I should paint a rainbow."

"That is kind of appropriate."

"Exactly."

I can't think of anything to say after that, and we end up simply smiling at one another for too long until suddenly it's awkward and I have to look away. I watch the waves hitting the shore and remind myself to breathe normally.

"Sophie," Caleb says quietly. "Why didn't you want to meet me in real life?"

The waves crash again and again while I consider exactly what to say. I should be honest with him. Or partially honest, at least. He'll keep asking otherwise.

"You said just now that you like me," I say, keeping my eyes on the water.

"I did say that."

"Well … I like you too. And I don't know if you mean it the same way I mean it, but there it is. I like you. And that's why it would be less complicated if we never met."

He says nothing for so long that eventually I'm forced to look at him. I find him leaning back against the bench, watching me with a smile.

"What?"

"Nothing," he says.

"Stop smiling like that."

"Like what?"

"Like I just said something good."

He pretends to suppress the smile—and does a terrible job of it. "You did say something good."

"I didn't. If you've been listening to everything else I've told you since we met, then you know it isn't something good. Or at least, it isn't something that matters."

"It all matters," he says.

179

I shake my head slowly and look down. His hand is on the bench between us. Right next to my hand. If I moved mine just a little bit, I'd be touching his. And I'm struck, suddenly, by how badly I want to. And I don't just want to hold his hand, I want to feel his arms around me, tight and secure. I want to rest my head on his shoulder. For so long he's been the person I turn to for everything. Always there on the other end of the Internet. Always ready to make me smile. And now he's only half a bench away from me, and I'm terrified and exhilarated at the same time.

My phones rings. Startled, I snatch it up immediately and find Sarah's face lighting up the screen. She's probably mad at me, but right now I'll happily take that over my terrifying feelings for Caleb.

"Sarah?" I answer, angling my body away from Caleb.

"Soph, what's going on?"

"I know, I know, I'm being terribly rude, and I'm so sorry. I didn't want to mess up this dinner for you."

"No, no, I'm just a little worried. You left with no explanation."

"I know, I'm sorry. That was inconsiderate of me." My fingers find the hem of my dress and begin folding it over and over.

"Are you okay? Is Caleb with you? He said you weren't feeling well and went outside to get some fresh air, and that he was going to keep you company. Mom's concerned. I told her pretty much what Caleb said, but I think she might come looking for you soon."

"Um, yes, Caleb's with me." I flatten the edge of my

180

dress, then begin rolling it up again. "I'm feeling okay now. We'll be back inside soon. You can tell Mom not to worry."

"Okay. Are you sure everything's all right?"

"Yes. Thanks, Sarah."

Caleb and I walk back to the restaurant together in silence. Not an uncomfortable silence, but not exactly an easy one either. Well, it's probably easy for him—judging by the grin he can't keep off his face—but it isn't easy for me. I keep my arms folded firmly over my chest. I might accidentally hold his hand otherwise, and that isn't allowed.

Dammit, I wish it was allowed.

I take a peek at him and find him watching me. His eyebrows rise slightly, expectantly. "Yes?"

Flipping heck, why is he waiting for *me* to say something? I've said my bit already. So all I say now is, "What?"

"Nothing."

"Nothing?"

"Yeah."

Well, this is quickly becoming the least intelligent conversation we've ever had.

"Okay, if you must know," he says, "I'm still marvelling at the fact that the amazing girl I've been chatting to online for the past few years is walking right next to me on a balmy summer's evening beside the beach. It's kinda perfect actually."

"Shut up," I murmur, looking away and trying not to smile as my face warms.

I'm never falling in love ever again.

It will never work out between the two of us.

We will only ever be friends.

These are all things I should be saying out loud, but I can't bring myself to. So instead we return to the restaurant in time to order dessert, and I spend the rest of the evening with a stupid, gooey grin on my face, feeling just a tiny bit like I'm floating.

I LIE AWAKE LATE ON THURSDAY NIGHT SENDING MESSAGES to LuminaireX. I start off with, **Is it weird if we still message each other now that we can actually talk in real life?** And after he responds with, **Well we can't talk in real life right now cos you're in another room**, we spend at least two hours discussing everything from the strange colour ties Aiden is making his groomsmen wear to the bit of plastic he found in his ice cream at the restaurant.

And neither of us mentions our discussion on the pier once. I sense Caleb might be waiting for me to bring it up first, which is fine because that means we'll never have to talk about it.

Friday. The day before the wedding. I feel as though we should be rushing around doing *something*, but we've collected all the decor items and all the favours and thank-you gifts. Everyone has their dress or suit and whatever else they'll be wearing tomorrow. Everything on the pin board is crossed off, and the flowers are only arriving later, and we can't get into the wedding venue until three this afternoon, so we somehow seem to be left with several hours in which we have nothing to do. I sense it's somewhat like the stillness before a massive storm—the storm in this case being the mad rush of decor set-up we'll need to start as soon as we get to the venue this afternoon—so I'm taking the morning to chill out in preparation for the craziness.

The breeze is cooler today than it's been all week, so we spread the picnic blankets on the grass outside. I lie on my stomach and scroll through emails and social media on my iPad. Caleb does something similar on his phone, occasionally reading out snippets of news to us, Aiden and Sarah look through their notes on exactly where all the decor items will be placed this afternoon, and Josh and Julia seem to be napping. I don't think Caleb's told anyone what we discovered last night—that he and I have actually known each other for years. I haven't told anyone either. It's not as though this revelation is a giant secret we have to keep, but it still feels so … new. So personal. I want to at least get used to the idea of Lex being right here in the flesh before casually mentioning to my family, "Hey, you know that artist I chat to online all the time …"

I browse some artist pages on Facebook and click

through to various recommended articles. I save pictures to Pinterest, watch the occasional video or two. "Oh, hey, look at this," I say, mainly to Caleb, since I doubt anyone else will be interested. "This lady paints on people and objects— literally *on* them and on the background around them—and it creates this optical illusion so that three-dimensional stuff looks two-dimensional. And then she photographs it."

"Why would someone want to do that?" Sarah murmurs, her attention still on her decor notes.

"I don't know, but it looks so cool. She uses these bold, broad strokes. All these colours on top of each other. It kinda tricks your brain into thinking there's no depth there, so a three-dimensional scene becomes a two-dimensional portrait. Look." I crawl over to Caleb's blanket and hand him my iPad. "We did some body painting for a school project last year, but it wasn't anything nearly this amazing."

"Oh, yeah, I know her," Caleb says.

"You've seen her stuff? But you never shared it with me."

"No, I mean I actually know her. I had the opportunity to be one of her subjects when she was experimenting early on. It was so cool."

My mouth drops open. "Seriously? Do you know *everyone?*"

He shrugs. "I'm a friendly guy."

I take my iPad back from him. "Well, anyway. Despite the fact that I'm probably the last person to discover this, I still thinks it's cool."

"It is," Caleb says, pushing himself up and smiling. It's

the same smile he's been giving me since the moment we met in the craft store, except now it gives me butterflies instead of annoying the heck out of me. "Want to try it?" he asks.

"What, this technique?" I gesture to the iPad. "Painting on ourselves?"

"Yeah. Do you have the right kind of paint?"

"Um, I think I might have some left from the body painting we did for school."

"Cool. Wanna do it?"

I picture myself in my tiny painting space in the corner of the garage with no one else but Caleb. Though I shouldn't, I say, "Okay."

We get up and walk through the house to the garage. Mom's in the kitchen organising snacks for this afternoon, and Dad's probably hiding somewhere practising his speech for tomorrow night. I switch the light on as we enter the garage. A dim, bare bulb at the centre of the ceiling flickers to life. In the corner of the garage, where my easel and paints are stored, I turn on another lamp. My little area is partially closed off by rusted metal shelving holding gardening supplies, Dad's toolbox, and various other home DIY materials.

Caleb looks around. "It's … cosy."

"You don't have to say anything nice."

"Look, at least it's something. I have to paint inside my apartment—"

"—which is great," I say. "I'd far rather use a room inside if Mom would let me."

"It's not so great when everyone else complains about the smell of chemicals."

"Well, people need to learn to appreciate the smell of paint," I say as I search through my supplies for the right kind. "So … can we work with just black and white, because that's all I've got."

"We can definitely work with just black and white." Caleb taps my iPad, bringing it back to life, and scrolls through the website I found. "Here's some stuff she's done with just black and white. We could try something like that."

"Cool. Okay, put that over there for reference." I point to the shelves.

Minutes later, we've each begun painting our own faces, using the side mirrors on Dad's car to help us. I've got the lid of an ice cream tub in one hand—with a blob of white and a blob of black on it—and a paintbrush in the other. "This is so ticklish," I say. "How do people keep from laughing while she's painting on them? They all look so professional in the videos on her website."

"They probably cut out all the giggly bits," Caleb says. He brushes black paint beneath his nose and adds, "Good thing I love the smell of paint."

"I love …" I cast my mind out and remember the storm from a few days ago. "I love the smell of rain on hot concrete on a summer's day."

"And the smell of freshly cut grass, which—"

"—everyone loves," I finish for him, because I'm pretty certain we've discussed this very thing at some point in the last two years. "Do you think we have enough time to do this properly?" I ask, straightening and looking at Caleb over the top of the car. "I mean, we could just paint our faces down to our shoulders, and then a background—I'm sure I've got a big board here somewhere that we could paint—and Jules can take a photo. It can be our first collab. What did you want to call us?"

"Ashlex."

"Yeah, that's right. This could be our first Ashlex work."

"Sure." He looks down and drags a broad stroke across the top of his chest. "Do you mind painting on your clothes?"

"Are you kidding?" I ask with a laugh. "I think I have more clothes with paint stains than without. Of course I don't mind covering this top in paint."

I look into the car's side mirror and paint my forehead and up into my hair. "Sarah would totally freak out if she came in here now. 'This isn't wedding productive!'" I say in high-pitched voice. "'You're wasting time!'"

"Sophie Henley, you're supposed to be supporting your sister at this time, not making fun of her." He walks around to my side of the car and dabs a spot of paint on my nose. "But since we've already begun this painting mess, we may as well continue."

"Hey, you can't interfere with my creative process."

"But you missed a spot. And you missed another one there." He dabs my cheek with his paintbrush.

"Well, you missed a spot too." I reach up and drag my paintbrush across the top of his head.

"Yeah, because I hadn't got there yet. Obviously."

"You do know that it's easier if we paint each other's faces, right?" Butterflies come to life inside my chest as the words leave my mouth. *What are you doing, Sophie?*

"Yes. That's why I came over here. I was having trouble seeing my whole face while bending over and peering into a car's side mirror."

I shrug, trying to keep things casual. "That's what happens when you have a big face."

He laughs. "Such a weak come-back." I stick my tongue out at him. "Want me to paint that?" he asks, his eyes sparkling with mirth.

"Definitely not! I may be fine with the smell of paint, but I don't think I'll enjoy the taste of it."

"Okay." He keeps grinning at me. "Wait, hang on, I just want to check those examples again." He walks back to my iPad on the shelf. "I want to see where she positions the black streaks for the shadows on the face."

I bend and look into the car window's reflection and paint another few strokes into my hairline before Caleb returns to my side. I straighten and face him. He loads his paintbrush from his palette—the lid of a margarine container—and paints a few strokes around my nose. Then slowly, hesitating a moment before he does it, he drags a streak of paint across my lower lip. And just like that, the atmosphere between us changes. It's charged, like the air before a storm. Like the anticipation of the sizzle and crack of that first lightning bolt.

I swallow. I raise my hand because I'm supposed to be painting him too, but I just ... can't. His eyes are on me, and his paintbrush is moving in soft strokes across my top lip, and I can't focus on anything else.

Caleb pulls the paintbrush back, and it hovers there, beside my face. Moving neither towards the paint nor to my skin. He hasn't said a word, and neither have I. I don't want to break the charged silence. He looks into my eyes and then back down at my lips, and I'm pretty sure—I'm pretty damn sure—he's leaning towards me.

I try to breathe. If he kisses me now, we are definitely going to end up with paint in our mouths, and I. Don't. Care. All my rules fly out the garage door because I don't care about them either. I don't think of how much this might end up hurting me. I don't think of *anything* except Caleb, Lex, the guy I've already fallen for, closing the space between us.

"Sophie? Soph, are you in here?"

I jerk backwards, sucking in a breath at the sound of Sarah's voice.

"Oh, there you—" Her eyes widen at the sight of us. "What on earth are you guys doing? We're supposed to be leaving in *ten minutes*."

"Ten minutes?"

"The venue is two hours away, Sophie!"

I take another step back from Caleb. "Yeah, but I thought we were only leaving after lunch."

"It is after lunch."

"Oh, crumbs. I had no idea."

"Sophie, there is *paint* in your *hair*," she says, her voice rising. "Are you crazy? That's never going to come out by tomorrow!"

"What? Sure it will." I mean, I think it will …

"It'll definitely come out," Caleb assures her. "If you go shower right now," he adds to me.

"Right. Yes." I lower my paintbrush and palette onto a shelf, grab my iPad, and hurry back into the house. Despite the fact that I've showered thousands of times before, I have to keep instructing myself on what to do.

Get your towel.

Get the clothes you're going to change into.

Walk downstairs.

Wait, you haven't got underwear. Back upstairs.

Downstairs again.

Turn the shower on.

Why? Because most of my brain is still stuck back there in the garage with Caleb, and all I want to do is drop everything, race back to that moment, and finish falling towards him.

Despite the fact that Caleb and I supposedly held everyone up while we were cleaning paint off ourselves, we arrive at the wedding venue in the Midlands a full ten minutes earlier than planned.

"Isn't it just the most beautiful place ever?" Sarah says as we climb from her car. She slowly turns on the spot. "I love that we can see the mountains from here. Love it, love it."

I follow her gaze, taking in the many trees, the hills sloping around us, the mountain peaks in the distance, and the beautiful old buildings. I can see why she loves it here so much, why she and Aiden chose this spot to begin their happily ever after.

"It's magical, Seh," Julia says as she and Josh look around. "Well done, you guys." She pats Aiden's arm.

Car doors swing shut behind us, and I look around, my eyes already searching for Caleb. We didn't end up in the same car, and I spent much of the journey here checking my phone to see if he'd sent a message. But he must have been chatting with everyone else in his car.

"Come on, let's get everything into the reception hall," Sarah says, steering me to the back of her car.

"Are we allowed in yet?" Julia asks.

Sarah hands me a box of vases. "We're only a few minutes early. I'm sure it's fine."

We all grab a box of something from the boot of Sarah's car and follow her around the side of one of the buildings towards what is clearly the reception building. Glass doors line the entirety of one side, opening up onto a sheltered terrace right beside a lake. "Oh, it's going to be so lovely," Julia says with a squeal.

The side doors are open, so we walk inside. It's an enormous room with rafters criss-crossing high above us. Tables and chairs are set out already with linen, cutlery and crockery in place. We lower our boxes to the floor.

"Mom, have you heard from Martine yet?" Sarah asks. "We need to get the flowers started as soon as possible."

"She's about twenty minutes away. We can get started with everything else."

"Wow, this is going to be quite a lot of work," Livi observes when she walks into the hall moments later. "Why weren't we allowed here this morning?"

"There was some other event in the smaller room next door," Sarah tells her, "and the venue coordinator said we'd be disturbing those people by carrying stuff in and out and blah, blah, blah. Anyway, we're here now, and I've planned exactly where everything's going to go, so we'll get it done in time. We can still have our chilled girls' evening." She turns to Aiden as he walks into the hall with another two boxes. "Oh, that stuff is actually for outside," she says. "And these two boxes here." She pushes them aside. "You remember where everything goes, right?" The two of them lean over her notepad together.

"Yeah, I remember that." Aiden points to something on the page. "And that as well. Yep, this all looks familiar."

"Great. Can you, Josh and Caleb take care of that? And when Nick arrives, he can help you guys."

Aiden gives her a quick kiss, then says, "Certainly."

He heads outside with his groomsmen, and after that, I don't see Caleb again.

"Well done, girls," Mom says when she's done hugging Sarah, Julia, Livi and me goodnight. "You've done an amazing job." Tears glisten in her eyes as she cups Sarah's cheek. "You're going to have the most beautiful and special day tomorrow." She kisses Sarah's forehead, then closes the bedroom door as she leaves.

The four of us, along with the two moms, are staying in a guest house near the wedding venue so we can get ready in private tomorrow without running the risk of bumping into Aiden or anyone else who isn't supposed to see the bride until the exact right moment. Another silly tradition, my brain reminds me, but for some reason I'm finding myself less and less bothered by silly traditions. Mom and Aiden's mother each have their own bedroom, but the four of us moved our beds so we could all sleep in one room. Sarah decided it would be fun that way.

Though we're all supposed to be getting an early night, the moment Mom leaves, we all pile onto Sarah's bed and continue chatting. "Oh my goodness, it was the biggest panic I've had in ages," Julia tells us with a laugh. "And I had to go two towns over to buy the pregnancy test because if I went to my local pharmacy, I would definitely have run into someone I know, and rumours of me being pregnant would have been circulating the community before I even peed on the darn stick."

I hug a cushion to my chest as I laugh. "So you're glad it was a false alarm?" I ask.

"Definitely. Josh and I are so not ready for babies yet."

"Yeah, that's a gigantic responsibility." Sarah leans back, tucks her legs beneath her, and looks at me. "So what's up with you and Caleb?"

I paste an innocent expression onto my face as I play with the tassels of the cushion. "What do you mean?"

She gives me a knowing smile. "You've refused to look at any guy in the past year. Now you can't stop smiling at Aiden's goofball best friend."

"Whom Mom is probably going to point out is too old for you at some point," Julia says. "Although it's not as though he acts like an adult," she adds with a thoughtful look, "so Mom's probably forgotten he's supposed to be one."

"You asked me to be nice to everyone, remember?" I say to Sarah. "So yeah. I smile at Caleb now. And everyone else."

Sarah laughs and shakes her head. "Nuh uh. You do not smile for anyone else the way you smile for him."

"It's really cute," Jules says, nudging my arm.

"And he's cute too," Livi adds. "So we totally don't blame you."

"Oh my goodness, please stop. You're the one who's getting married tomorrow, Sarah. Shouldn't we be talking about you?"

"No. I've spent far too much time talking about myself recently. Besides," she adds, "I'm super nervous about tomorrow, and talking about it does not relax me *at all*. So I want to know what's going on with you guys instead."

"Well you already know that Josh and I aren't having babies for at least another year," Julia says, "so that's my bit."

"And you all know my news," Livi says with a giant smile on her face. "Well, my *suspicions*, I should say. About Adam maybe, possibly having purchased a certain ring."

"Which you should know nothing about," Julia scolds. "These things are supposed to be a surprise."

"I'm sorry, it was an accident! I didn't know he was going to be at the mall that day. Inside that jewellery shop. For a long time …"

Julia narrows her eyes at Livi. "How long were you spying on him?"

"Anyway," Sarah interrupts. "So now we're down to you, Soph. Come on. Spill."

With a sigh, I relent. I could evade their questions for longer if I choose to, but a tiny part of me wants to be that girl who gets giggly and excited about a guy. I had that once upon a time, and I thought it ruined me, but now that it's happening again, I can't seem to make myself step away. Everything's upside down. My feelings are all over the place, my rules are going up in flames, and now that someone's giving me a chance to say it out loud, I can't seem to keep it in. "Fine," I say. "Caleb is … Caleb is Lex."

Sarah's eyes widen. "Wait, what?"

"Who's Lex?" Julia and Livi ask at the same time.

"This artist guy Sophie's always chatting with online," Sarah tells them. "Like *always*."

"Yeah." I hug the cushion closer to my chest.

"How is—Wait." Sarah's eyes squeeze shut for a moment as she shakes her head. "Caleb is Lex? Seriously?"

"Yeah."

"So you've been in an internet relationship with Caleb?" Livi asks.

"Not like *that*. Just a friendship. And I didn't know it was him until last night."

"Oh, at the dinner," Julia says. "Now it makes sense why you suddenly got up and left."

"And he went after you," Livi adds.

"Wait, hang on," Sarah says, raising her hands. "I'm still trying to make sense of this. I know Caleb does all this fantasy art, and he has this page on Facebook that often comes up in my feed. The Luminaire Artist. So where does the name Lex come from?"

"On Artster, where I first got in contact with him, his name is LuminaireX. I shortened that to Lex."

Sarah's eyebrows climb up her forehead. "Oh my goodness. Are you kidding me? You never made the connection?"

"No! How was I going to make the connection? You know I'm hardly ever on Facebook."

"This is insane," she says.

"I know." Insanely amazing, but I manage to keep myself from adding that.

"So how long have you guys actually known each other?" Julia asks.

"Pretty much as long as Sarah and Aiden have known each other."

"Wow. That's so weird."

"And what exactly was happening in the garage today?" Sarah asks.

"The garage?" Julia repeats.

"They were painting each other," Sarah tells her. "But I walked in just as—"

"—things were getting kinky?" Livi asks with a mischievous grin.

"Oh my goodness, guys. We are going to bed. Now." I throw the cushion at Sarah before climbing off her bed and heading to mine. "Beauty sleep, remember?"

"But the story was just getting good," Livi complains as she bounces onto her bed.

"That was the *end* of the story." I pull my covers back and climb into bed. The cooler Midlands air means we'll get to enjoy a night of snuggling beneath our duvets instead of kicking them off as we overheat. "I haven't even spoken to Caleb since the painting thing. We were all too busy decorating the venue, remember?"

"That wasn't the end of your story," Sarah says as she leans over to turn off the lamp. "An interlude, perhaps, but definitely not the end."

We fall into silence after a few more whispers and giggles. The painting scene plays over and over in my mind, and I'm pretty sure my stupidly wide smile is still on my face when I fall asleep.

The wedding is perfect. Sarah is without a doubt one of the most beautiful brides on earth, and I have to bite my shuddering lip when I reach the front of the chapel, look over my shoulder, and see her taking her first steps down the aisle. Despite the fact that I've spent so many months rolling my eyes at the very mention of this occasion, now that it's here, I am completely swept up in the emotion of it all. I blink away tears during the vows, shout out in celebration when Tim pronounces Sarah and Aiden husband and wife, and toss as many petals into the air as I can when they emerge from the chapel at the end of the ceremony.

As laughter, hugs and congratulations sweep throughout the gathering outside the chapel, Caleb appears beside me, leans closer for just a moment, and whispers, "It's never felt so good to lose a bet, has it?"

My beaming smile is all the answer he needs. I almost throw my arms around him right then and there, but I'm intercepted by one of Mom's aunts who pulls me into a perfume-infused hug and gives me the whole 'you're looking so grown-up now' talk. Instead of reminding her that it's been five years since she last visited, so *obviously* I'm grown-up now, I politely thank her and answer all her questions. And I do it all with a genuine smile.

What with all the photographs that have to be taken, and all the relatives that have to be greeted, I don't get a chance to speak to Caleb until we're all told to go inside the reception venue and sit down. And then he ends up on the other side of the bridal party table, stuck in conversation with Livi and Adam. Julia moves her chair closer to mine and tells me all about how a small child was crawling around at the back of the chapel during the ceremony and knocked over a candle. "The carpet caught alight, and the kid's dad quickly covered it up with his jacket, and we didn't know anything was happening!"

"Please don't tell Sarah that story," I say through my laughter. "She thinks everything was perfect."

"Well, everything important *was* perfect." She reaches for my hand and squeezes it. "It's your turn next, Soph."

I roll my eyes at her silly statement, but I can't help looking across the table. I catch Caleb's eye, and his lips stretch into a smile just for me. I push my chair back, planning to move around to his side of the table until the reception proceedings begin, but the tinkling of a spoon against glass makes me look around. The MC, Aiden's groomsman Nick, stands at the edge of the dance floor near the DJ's table with a microphone in one hand. He asks everyone to stand before directing our attention towards the closed hall doors. "Everyone," he calls out just as the doors are thrown open, "I'd like to introduce you to the brand new Mr and Mrs Harrison."

After the speeches, which are lovely, and the starter and main, which are delicious, we get to the part of the evening I've been looking forward to the most. The part where I will finally have Caleb all to myself.

The dancing.

A week ago, I would have called anyone who told me this crazy. Absolutely bonkers. No way would I be looking forward to the *dancing* part of this evening. And I'm still not entirely keen on the idea of moving around a dance floor with over a hundred pairs of eyes on me. But if this is what it takes to get a few uninterrupted minutes with Caleb tonight, then I'll gladly do it. Besides, I remind myself. Everyone will be looking at Sarah and Aiden.

We perch on the edge of our chairs as the first dance begins. When the moment arrives for us to join Sarah and Aiden, I stand along with the rest of the bridal party and walk onto the dance floor. My heart races with equal parts nervousness and anticipation. I take Caleb's outstretched hand and place my other hand on his shoulder. I hear

Lucille's voice in my head counting us in, which makes me want to laugh

I don't look over Caleb's shoulder this time. I look straight into his eyes, which causes warmth to spread across my insides and burn my cheeks. But the lights are dimmed in here, so I doubt anyone aside from Caleb can see me blushing.

We're almost at the end of the dance when I say, "Are you happy you won?"

He chuckles. "I'm happy you're happy."

I shake my head. "Such a cheesy answer."

"And, of course, I'm happy that you now have to dance the rest of the night with me," he adds.

As we walk, walk, pivot around, I say, "Well, I have a secret to tell you." Walk, walk, side, tap. "Even if there was no bet, I'd keep dancing with you for the rest of the night."

"Oh, the cheesiness is killing me!" If we weren't still dancing, he'd probably be miming stabbing himself in the heart. Instead, we're suddenly dancing way too close to Livi and Nick.

"Eek, watch out!" I say, squeezing Caleb's shoulder. He adds in an extra pivot step, swinging us out of the way and narrowly avoiding a collision with Nick and Livi. I try to control my laughter as I say, "Excellent save. I don't think Sarah even noticed."

The music changes, bringing the first dance to an end, and a lively, fun beat fills the hall. "Get ready to dance until you drop!" Caleb says, twirling me around and around as everyone else joins in the dancing.

We do indeed dance until we drop. We dance to every single song until Nick takes the microphone and announces that it's time for Sarah and Aiden to cut the cake. Caleb spins me towards the edge of the dance floor, where I tumble into the nearest empty chair and remove my shoes.

Sarah and Aiden cut through their wedding cake together and everyone applauds. Then roars of laughter fill the hall as Aiden tries to smear a piece of cake across Sarah's face. Sarah must have had some warning, though, because she dodges out the way, then flattens a piece of cake on top of his head. Then she shrieks and dashes away into the crowd of guests with Aiden chasing after her.

Beside me, Caleb is bent over he's laughing so much. "She did it," he gasps. "I warned her … about Aiden trying that … and told her she must get him back for it."

I take his arm and pull him down onto the chair next to mine. "Sit down before you hurt yourself," I say when I've managed to stop laughing.

He sighs and leans back in the chair, wiping tears away. As everyone starts queuing at the buffet tables for dessert, he says, "I think I need some cool air after all that dancing. Want to take a walk outside?"

I almost say, 'I'll go anywhere you want,' but I manage to catch myself before I become completely corny. *Seriously?* I add silently. *Who are you and what have you done with the real Sophie?* Caleb's still waiting for an answer, though, so I smile at him and say, "Sure."

I leave my shoes under our table and walk outside barefoot to give my feet a break. We cross the terrace and step onto the grass. The evening air is cool, but a welcome relief from the stuffy interior of the reception hall.

Caleb pushes his hands into his pockets and looks out across the lake. "Did Aiden tell you we drove back to Durban this morning?

"What? No. Did someone forget something?"

"Yep." He looks at me with a guilty expression. "That someone was me, and the thing I forgot was the box with the rings."

My mouth drops open. "Seriously? Oh my goodness. Can you imagine Sarah's reaction if she'd walked down the aisle and only *then* you realised you'd left the rings behind?"

"Yes. I imagined her reaction a number of times. Mostly while feeling insanely grateful that I remembered the rings before it was too late to go back for them."

"How did you forget them?" I place my hands behind my back and lace my fingers together, since I have nothing else to do with my hands and it's starting to feel awkward. "Aren't the rings supposed to be somewhere near the top of the packing list for a best man?"

Caleb sighs. "I put them in a drawer in the room I was staying in at your parents' house so they didn't get lost amongst all the clothes I was moving around my suitcase every day. And then … I forgot to put them back."

"Thank goodness home was only two hours away."

"Yeah." He pauses, then says, "Anything exciting happen with you girls this morning?"

Nothing nearly as exciting as what almost happened in the garage yesterday, I want to say. But if he isn't bringing it up, then I'm not sure I should bring it up either. "Other than having my neck burnt with a hair curler? Not really."

"Oh, ouch." He takes a casual step closer to me and adds, "This is the part where you pull your hair aside and show me the burn on your neck, which gives me an excuse to move even closer to you and maybe brush my fingers against your skin while I examine the burn with great concern."

A shiver rushes down my arms and up my neck and into my hair. But despite my blush and the smile straining at my lips, I don't play along. "Well I can't say that now that you've suggested it, can I? That would make things far too easy for you. You'll have to come up with something else just as smooth. Like …" I look away from him and drag my right foot back and forth across the grass, letting it tickle the sole of my foot. "Like commenting on the fact that we didn't get to finish our first collaboration yesterday."

"Indeed," he says, moving a little closer, "that would be very smooth."

I peek up at him and find an amused smile upon his lips. I wait to see if he'll say anything else, and at that point, it begins to rain. Not the deluge of a storm, but the gentle patter of droplets.

Caleb starts laughing and shakes his head. "Turns out nature is smoother than either of us." I give him a quizzical look. He reaches out and takes my hand. His fingers slide between mine, and another shiver races up my arm. I expect him to pull me back towards the terrace now that we're getting wet, but instead he faces me and says, "You know why it's raining, right?"

I give a small shake of my head. "Why?"

"Because you've always wanted to be kissed in the rain, and I've always wanted to kiss you, so *clearly*—" one side of his mouth stretches up "—this moment is meant to be."

It's possible I've never been as happy as I am right now. "You haven't *always* wanted to kiss me," I say, trying to make the moment last as long as possible. "You didn't even know I existed until two years ago."

He lifts one shoulder. "Kinda feels like always to me." His hand—the one that isn't entwined with mine—brushes the edge of my jaw. His thumb runs along my rain-dampened lips. I can't seem to breathe properly, and my blood rushes so quickly through my veins that I wonder if I might actually pass out before he kisses me.

Caleb doesn't move any closer, though, which I'm pretty sure means he's waiting for me. After all, I'm the one who's sworn never to fall in love again. *Good thing*, my heart whispers to me, *that you fell for him a long time ago.*

I toss caution to the wind, grasp the front of his shirt, and pull myself towards him. His lips are soft and wet, and then fierce and powerful as our hands detach and he pulls me against him. Rain trickles down my face and into my mouth and over my tongue and his tongue. His fingers slide into my hair and my hands press against his back and the rain keeps on coming and our lips keep on kissing. And even though part of me is utterly terrified, I know it's okay that I'm falling.

Because it's with him.

23

JUST BEFORE MIDNIGHT, WE ALL STAND IN A LONG LINE waving sparklers as we send the bride and groom on their way. After that, some guests head off to wherever they're staying for the night, while others carry on dancing. I can't bear to wear my heels any longer, but my feet are getting cold, so I tell Caleb I'm going to fetch a pair of pumps from my room. Since he's being all gentlemanly—or, more likely, because he wants to steal another kiss without my parents watching over us—he offers to walk with me.

The rooms aren't too far from the reception hall. After getting the key from Dad, who kindly moved everyone's bags from the guest house and into the right rooms while we were all getting ready this morning, Caleb and I track down the door with the correct number.

"Do you know who you're sharing with?" Caleb asks as I step inside and search the wall for a light switch.

"One of my cousins." I find the light switch and click it on. "Who are you sharing a room with?"

"Nick. The other groomsman. We shared last night as well."

"Ooh, how romantic." I walk to the bed beside the window and unzip my suitcase.

"Yeah. He snores. I almost strangled him in his sleep." At the sight of my raised eyebrows, he adds, "Just kidding. I chucked a pillow at him, but that was it."

I sit on the edge of the bed to put my shoes on, and suddenly I'm just too tired to get up. "You know what? I'm actually just going to go to bed now. This day has really taken it outta me."

Caleb crosses the room and sits beside me on the bed. He raises my hand and kisses it. "That's fine. Want me to stay and keep you company until your cousin gets back? I assume she won't be too much longer."

I tilt my head to the side and say, "Do *you* want to stay and keep me company?"

A faint flush appears in his cheeks. "Well, it's *possible* that I might be looking for any excuse to spend just a few more minutes with you. Or as many minutes as you'll allow me."

I close the space between us and press my lips against his for several moments. When I lean back, I say, "Well they're going to be a boring few minutes, I'm afraid, because I really need to shower. And no, that is *not* an invitation for you to join me," I add as I see him open his mouth to comment.

He smiles instead. "You know me so well, Angel Ash."

"Yeah, yeah."

209

I drag my suitcase into the bathroom, close the door, and spend a while washing the crunchy bird's nest feeling out of my hair. Then I pull on boxers and a sleep shirt—slightly better than a tank top—and walk back out to find Caleb lying on my bed with one leg crossed over the other. He isn't sleeping, but he doesn't appear to be doing anything other than staring at the ceiling.

"What are you thinking about?" I ask as I sit beside him and rub a towel over my wet hair.

"I don't know. Lots of random stuff, I guess. Kissing in the rain, that dead bug on the ceiling, the fact that I haven't uploaded a new artwork to Artster in a while, how lucky I am that I found you in real life."

I poke him with my foot. "You're just trying to earn another few minutes in this room."

"Maybe. Did it work?"

I shrug. "Maybe."

As it turns out, he earns more than a few minutes. Despite my exhaustion, we keep talking and talking and talking some more, and when Caleb picks up his phone to check a message notification, he says, "Flip, that went fast."

"What?"

"The time." He turns his phone around so I can see the numbers.

"Oh my goodness, how is it almost two a.m.? Wait, where's Shirley?"

"Shirley?"

"My cousin. The one I'm sharing with tonight."

We stare at each other for a moment before Caleb starts

laughing. "Well, I can think of one answer."

I roll my eyes. "No way. Shirley isn't like that. She wouldn't spend the night with a guy she randomly met at a wedding."

"Okay, so should we send out a search party then?"

"Hang on." I climb off the bed and go to my suitcase. I haven't checked my phone since I packed it away this morning while we were getting dressed at the guest house. I figured I probably wouldn't need it during my sister's wedding.

I fish the phone out of one of the inside pockets and take a look at the screen. After scrolling past a few social media notifications, I see a missed call and a text message from Shirley, both from just over two hours ago. With a sigh, I say, "It's okay. No search party needed." I walk back to the bed and turn my phone to face Caleb so he can see the message.

Shirley: Hey, cuz! Couldn't find you to say goodbye. I'm supposed to be sharing with you tonight, but my mom said there's space at the house she and my dad and Aunt Maggie and Uncle Tom are staying at. Enjoy having the room to yourself!

"Oh, well that's a relief." He yawns, then adds, "I guess I should probably get back to my own room."

I nod. "Probably." I pause and bite my lip. "Or, you know, since you're already in a bed, you could just … stay there."

He hesitates, then slowly says, "I could."

"But you'll stay in this bed. And I'll stay in that one. Because that's what's appropriate."

He pushes himself up. "Soph, I don't ever want to make you uncomfortable. If you'd rather I go back to—"

"No, it's fine. I'm just letting you know the rules." I climb into the bed that was meant for Shirley and reach for the lamp.

"Well, uh, since I'm staying," Caleb says, "do you mind if I shower quickly? I got pretty sweaty on the dance floor."

I remove my hand from the lamp without switching it off. "Sure, okay."

I'm so tired I almost fall asleep while Caleb's in the shower, but I hear the bathroom door open when he's done and crack one eye open as he walks to the other bed. "Feel better?" I murmur.

"Much." He pulls back the duvet and climbs beneath it. "Night, Angel Sophie."

I smile and reach sleepily for the lamp switch. "Night, Caleb."

The room is plunged into darkness, and instead of falling immediately into the oblivion of sleep, I suddenly feel more awake. I can hear Caleb turning over, hear him fluffing up his pillow. He stops moving, but I'm still awake. Thoughts of what's going to happen when he leaves Durban in two days' time begin to creep in at the edges of my mind. I force them out instantly. I refuse to entertain those thoughts for a second. That's future-me's problem. Right now I'll simply lie hear listening to his steady breaths, remembering his lips pressing against mine, his arms around me, his whispers against my rain-drenched hair …

Oh, what the heck.

I push the duvet back and climb out of bed. I tiptoe across the small space, carefully pull back Caleb's duvet, and climb in next to him. "Um …" He raises his head slightly. "I think I'm probably supposed to remind you now that this is a complete violation of your own rules."

"Shush, I'm just … cold. Normally I have Scrunch to keep me warm." And in the middle of summer, I push him off the bed every night, but I don't need to add that.

"Did you just compare me to your dog?"

"Yes. Scrunch is amazing. You should be honoured to be compared to him."

"So … this is happening?"

"Yes, but you still have to behave."

"Of the two of us, you're the only one who's mis-behaved so far."

I bite my lip to keep from giggling. I'm supposed to be fast asleep by now, and instead I'm lying here right next to the person I have the most crazy insane feelings for in the whole world with a ridiculous grin on my face.

He slips his arm around me and pulls me against his chest, and warm happiness erupts inside me. "I'm never gonna sleep now," he whispers into my hair.

I place my hand over his. *Neither am I*, I think, but I don't say anything. I close my eyes and listen to him breathing, and at some point, my thoughts slide into dreams …

"SOPHIE HENLEY, WHAT IS GOING ON?"

I wake with a start at the sound of my mother's voice. I feel the warm body lying right beside me, and I remember everything from last night—and then I see my mother towering over the side of the bed. I push myself up and rub my scratchy eyes. "Jeez, Mom, what are you doing in here?"

"What am I—What is *he* doing in here?"

Behind me, Caleb clears his throat. "Um, hi, Mrs H."

"Don't you dare Mrs H. me. I actually liked you, young man. Now what am I supposed to think when I find you in bed with my youngest daughter?"

I scratch the back of my neck and say, "Would you believe me if I told you it was my fault?"

Mom folds her arms over her chest and fixes me with her most unimpressed stare. "Please leave the room, Caleb," she says without looking away from me. "I would like to speak to my daughter."

Caleb—who slept in his suit pants and a vest he must have had on underneath his shirt—climbs past me off the bed, retrieves his shirt and jacket from the top of my suitcase, and heads for the door with one last apologetic glance in my direction.

I sit on the edge of my bed and push my hand through my tangled hair while Mom begins pacing. "Mom," I say to her. "The only thing that happened in this bed last night was sleeping."

"Well if that's the case, I'm not sure why you couldn't each do it in your own beds."

I let out a long sigh. "We just … stayed up late. We were talking. I was waiting for Shirley to come back and I didn't see her message about staying somewhere else until, like, two this morning. We were both so tired already, so I just told Caleb to stay."

"And at what point did he climb into your bed?"

I look at her. "I climbed into his bed, actually."

"Sophie!"

"What?"

"He's seven years older than you!"

I throw my hands up. "And the sky is blue, and our pool needs to be cleaned. Why are we tossing random facts around?"

"Don't pretend like this is nothing when it is."

"Don't make this into a big deal when it isn't," I counter.

"Sophie—" She cuts herself off and breathes out sharply through her nose, shaking her head. "I've given you a lot of leeway. I've been tolerant of your mood swings and your rudeness and your lack of effort for your schoolwork, because I know what you've been through, and I know you had to cope with it in whatever way you could. But we have *never* allowed this sort of thing. Sleepovers with boys are absolutely out of the question."

"Mom," I say, but apparently she hasn't finished yet.

"I'm just … I'm worried about you, Soph. This is your first relationship since … since Braden. And if Caleb's so much older than you, it's probably not going to end well."

I fold my arms over my chest. "Can I point out a few things? In a reasonable and polite manner, of course. I'm not trying to be rude here."

Mom sighs. "Fine."

"Firstly, who said Caleb and I are in a relationship? Secondly, he has the maturity level of a sixteen year old, so I don't know why you're concerned about the age difference. And thirdly … don't I get to make my own decisions now that I'm eighteen?"

"You've known this guy for a week, Sophie. A *week*! That's it!"

"Actually I've known him for two years."

Mom pulls her head back, her eyebrows drawing together. "What are you talking about?"

I close my eyes for a moment, thinking of the quickest way to explain this. "Sarah met Aiden. They connected on Facebook. Sarah saw some art on Facebook she thought I'd like, so she shared it with me. I connected with that artist on a different art site. Two years later, it turns out that artist is

Aiden's friend Caleb."

Mom blinks. "Caleb is that artist you're always messaging?"

"Yes."

Mom pauses with a frown on her face and her mouth half open. She stares at nothing for a while, clearly trying to process what I've just told her. Then she blinks and shakes her head and says, "That doesn't change the fact that you've behaved completely inappropriately with Caleb. I obviously can't control your actions when you're away from home, but this will not be happening under our roof, do you understand?"

With a sigh, I say, "Yes. I understand."

"And since Caleb is leaving for the next part of his vacation tomorrow," Mom adds, "this shouldn't be a problem."

Thanks for reminding me, Mom.

She leaves my room, and I try desperately to cling to some of the happiness I've gathered over the past week. Moments later, my door opens again. Caleb sneaks inside and shuts the door—making it suddenly a whole lot easier for me to feel happy. I start laughing. "Do you have a death wish?"

"Maybe." He walks towards me. "Maturity level of a sixteen year old, huh?"

"You were listening?"

"Of course I was listening. It's been ages since I've got into trouble with a girl's parents. Makes me feel young again." He bats his eyes innocently. "Like a sixteen year old."

"Shut up."

"Oh come on, that was fun. Admit it."

"If you think that was fun, why don't you move into my attic with me in my parents' house? That'll really get you into trouble."

He laughs, then brushes my cheek with his knuckles and leans forward to press his lips against mine. "I just came back to give you a kiss. And to say that I've thought of where you should go to begin your travel adventures."

I lean back on my hands. "Where? With you?"

"Yes. However did you guess?"

I roll my eyes. "Didn't you say I know you by now?"

"I guess I did. So what do you think?"

"I … I don't know. That might actually be …"

"The best plan ever?"

My lips stretch into a grin. "Yes."

He squeezes my hand and places another quick kiss on my lips. "We can chat about it later when we get back to Durban. Or tomorrow before I leave."

"Okay."

He leaves with a smile, and I flop back onto the bed, holding onto this promise of happiness.

Sunday turns out to be another crazy family day. Sarah and Aiden might be off on their honeymoon, but most of the people who travelled from afar to celebrate their wedding are still around. Mom ends up inviting everyone back to our place after we've all left the wedding venue, which means we have at least twenty extra people hanging out at our house all afternoon and evening. And Caleb, being the super friendly guy that he is, makes friends with all of them.

I end up annoyed that I can't sit and talk to him properly, but he promises me we'll go out for breakfast tomorrow morning, just the two of us, before he leaves. "Are you asking me out on a date, LuminaireX?"

He kisses me then, right there in the garden where anyone who happens to be looking our way might see. "Yes, I am," he says when he's done. "Are you saying yes?"

I try to hide my flushed cheeks, but it's no use. "I am."

I head back inside to get some work done. Julia collides into me in the lounge with a squeal and says, "*Now* try to tell me there's no more to the story between you and Caleb."

I bite my lip as my smile threatens to take over my face again. "Fine, there may be something going on between us. But I'm not talking about it now because I have work to do."

She hugs me and says, "You'd better tell me everything soon."

As I leave the lounge, I notice Mom watching me. My smile slips when I see her deep frown, but I refuse to feel guilty about this. Just because I broke a rule and slept in the same bed with Caleb doesn't mean he's the wrong guy for me.

What about your other rule? a quiet, insidious voice at the back of my mind asks. *The promise you made yourself to never fall in love again?*

I tell my internal voice to get lost.

On Monday morning as Dad gets to work on clearing his study, he asks me to return the picnic blankets we borrowed from the church.

"Cool, Caleb and I can drop them off on our way to breakfast."

Dad's eyebrows twitch upward, but he nods without

saying anything. I wonder what Mom's told him about Caleb and me.

Fifteen minutes later, I park Dad's car outside the church. We both walk inside, and Caleb hangs out in the front office making friends with someone while I take the picnic blankets through the hall, past a knitting club, to the store room behind the stage. On my way out, I'm stopped by one of the knitting ladies, Mrs Mulder, who obviously remembers me from before I stopped coming to church. She asks me to tell her everything about the wedding. I give her the brief version of how beautiful Sarah was, what a special ceremony we had, how lovely the venue was, and how much fun we all had. I give the sweet old lady a hug and turn to leave—

—and see the woman standing in the doorway watching me.

Crap it.

It's Braden's mother. I see her every now and then around town, but I always try to avoid her. I have no idea what she's doing here, but there's no way I'll be able to leave without saying something. I feel sick all of a sudden. Sick and cold and guilty.

"Hi, Sharon," I say awkwardly.

"Hello, Sophie."

"Um, how are you?"

"Coping," she says. "I hear your sister just got married."

"Yes, this past weekend."

"How lovely for your family," she says quietly. Bitterly.

I think about running, but I can't leave without saying

something about *him*.

"Sharon, I—I know that this time of year is sad, but … I … It's a beautiful day. Maybe … maybe you can sit outside in your garden. I know how much you love gardening, so maybe that will … help." *Stop talking, Sophie. Just stop.*

Sharon's eyes narrow, and she peers more closely at me. "Today is a beautiful day?" she repeats.

My breath quickens as anxiety eats away at my insides.

"You've forgotten, haven't you," she says. "You don't know what today is."

"Today?" It can't be. I know what she's getting at, but it can't be. It can't be today. Because today is … I remember the date of the wedding first, because that's the date we've been working up to for so long. I add on two days and—

Holy freaking crap.

It's today. How could I forget? How, how, *how* could I forget that today is the first anniversary?

You know how, says that insidious voice. *You know the distractions you've allowed in.*

"I-I'm sorry," I stammer and step past Sharon.

Tears ache behind my eyes, begging to be shed, and for the first time in many months, I let them fall. Stupid, stupid me. What was I thinking? That I could actually have a happily ever after with Caleb? That he'd never grow tired of me and leave me heartbroken? That I could actually be *enough* for him?

I don't see him near the front office, so hopefully he's waiting outside near the car. I swipe at the tears streaking down my cheeks. *Breathe, breathe, breathe, Sophie. Just breathe.*

I find Caleb leaning against the side of the car. "Hey, there you—Soph, what's wrong?" He pushes away from the car and comes towards me.

I hold a hand up, stopping him. "I can't." I shake my head. "I just … I can't do this."

"WHAT ARE YOU TALKING ABOUT?" CALEB ASKS, TRYING TO put his arms me. "What happened."

I push his hands away. I pace back and forth alongside the car, breathing deeply until I've got the tears under control and can speak again. *Get it out*, I tell myself. *Just get it all out.*

"Last year, a few weeks before Christmas, exactly one year ago from today, m-my ex-boyfriend … committed suicide. That's how our relationship ended. We had this up-and-down, super intense, multiple-breakups, one-and-a-half-year relationship, and then he killed himself." My face scrunches up again as I fight against the tears. I take a gasp of air and continue. "And I tried s-so hard to save him. Over and over again, no matter how many times he broke my heart, I just kept on loving him. I thought somehow that would be enough. I thought I could help him to be happy,

224

but I couldn't do it. I wasn't enough. I gave *absolutely everything* inside me, and it wasn't enough for him."

"Sophie—"

"And I know it d-doesn't sound like it right now, but I h-have actually dealt with this. I've seen a counsellor. I've done the therapy thing. I've moved on with life. But in my own way. And my own way means none of this." I wave my hand between the two of us. "I can't do this. I refuse to go through that kind of heartbreak again. I can't put my heart out there only to discover once again that it isn't enough for someone."

"You … you think you're not enough for me?"

"Caleb …" I cover my face with my hands. "No, I am not enough for you. I know what kind of person you are, and the kind of person that *I* am will just end up ruining you."

"That's complete nonsense. You *are* enough for me. You're exactly what I want and what I need. That's what I wanted to tell you when you asked about the click thing."

I sniff and lower my hands. "The click thing?"

"You asked what 'magic click element' I've been searching for in the right girl. The answer is *you*. It's been you for ages, ever since I woke up one day and realised that of all the people I interact with, both in real life and online, you were the one I wanted to hear from most. But you weren't interested in meeting me, so I figured I'd have to find someone else. I hoped there might be someone out there just like you. But there isn't. *You* are what I'm looking for. *You* are enough for me."

I shake my head. "I won't be. I'm not a happy person, Caleb, and I don't want to make you unhappy."

"That's a lie. You *can* be happy when you allow yourself to be. I've seen proof of that this week."

"That—that wasn't real."

"It was! Don't lie to me."

"I'm not lying."

"Why can't you just let me make you happy?"

"Because I don't deserve it!"

And there it is. The deep-down, ugly truth of it all. The truth that taints everything good in my life. Caleb is silent for way too long before speaking. "So let me get this straight," he says quietly. "Your ex-boyfriend killed himself because you apparently weren't enough to make him happy, and because of that, *you* don't deserve to be happy?"

I press my lips together and stare at the ground. This conversation needs to end now. I need to walk away. Walk away and get back to the life I had before Caleb showed up. Except … I'll never get back to that life again because Lex will be gone. Dammit, this is a mess.

"Don't you realise how utterly ludicrous that is?" Caleb says gently. "Didn't your counsellor tell you that?"

She did, and maybe I even believed it for a while, but seeing Sharon just now …

"Your counsellor must have told you that his death wasn't your fault, right?" Caleb bends a little, trying to get me to look him in the eye. "Right?" he says again.

"Yes."

"But you've decided you know better?"

"I do know better!" I shout. "You weren't there just now. You didn't see Braden's mother. The way she looks at me. The way she blames me. The way her eyes say, 'How dare you be happy when my son is dead?'"

"That's …" Caleb closes his eyes for a moment and lets out a long breath. "This whole thing is horrible. And tragic. I get that. I can't begin to imagine what she must have gone through, and what she's still going through. But it isn't fair of her to blame you."

"Caleb—"

"And I think you know that. So if you really are over him, then please don't make this about him."

"Caleb, you can't say things like—"

"Why not? Am I being disrespectful? This isn't about him anymore. This is about you and me and the fact that *we have something*, Sophie. We do. I know you know that."

"That doesn't matter! Even if I believed that I deserve happiness and never have to feel guilty about Braden ever again, that doesn't mean that what you and I have will last."

"Why not? I'm not going to leave you, Soph."

"Yes you are! You're leaving *today*."

He shakes his head. "You know that's not what I mean. That's temporary. I can live anywhere. You can live anywhere. We could live in the exact same place if we wanted to. We've been hanging out online for almost two years, and in that time I've never got tired of you. I've never stopped communicating. I've never stopped wishing I could meet you in real life."

"But that was different! This—a real-life relationship

227

where we have to actually *live life together* instead of just chatting about it—is the kind of thing where you could eventually decide it isn't working out between us."

He throws his arms up. "Well that's a risk you have to take if you want to be a human being living in this world."

"Maybe I'm not willing to take that risk."

He steps back, looking for all the world as if I just slapped him. "Well," he says quietly. "Given my fear of choosing the wrong person to spend my life with and ending up just like my parents, I'd say it's a good thing we got this out of the way before it ended in a mess for both of us."

"Caleb …"

"No, Sophie. Don't try to placate me. Don't try to make this better. Do you have any idea how fervently and wholeheartedly I believed you were the right one for me?"

"Caleb—"

"How could I possibly be wrong, I thought. And yet I am. I've been wrong all this time. Because if you really were the right one, then you'd be willing to take a risk for me. You'd be willing to trust me, to trust *us*."

He waits one last time for me to say something. But there isn't anything else for me to say, so I simply press my lips together and will myself not to cry. He turns and walks away down the road, and I don't call out to him to come back.

I HIDE AWAY WITH MY BROKEN HEART, WORKING DILI-gently on current projects and actively seeking out new clients, until Isabelle finds me in the afternoon of Christmas Eve. I'm sitting at my desk taking a brief break and staring at Artster yet again. Staring at the messages section where there is still nothing new from LuminaireX. I was wrong when I thought I could never really lose him. Wrong when I thought that it wasn't real just because it was all Internet-based. Of course it was real, and now I've lost it all.

I look up at the sound of footsteps on my stairs. Moments later, Isabelle appears in my doorway. She doesn't say anything, just leans against the doorframe and looks at me.

"I failed again, didn't I," I say quietly. "I totally failed at being a friend."

"Maybe," she says. "Maybe not. Maybe if you tell me

what's wrong without me having to pry it from you, then you won't have failed completely. And maybe, hopefully, you'll find that talking to someone actually helps you feel a little better."

I push my wheeled chair away from my desk, stand up, and walk to my bed. I slump against the pillows, and Isabelle takes up her position at the foot of the bed.

"Remember Lex?" I say.

"Of course."

"Remember Caleb?"

"Yeah."

"They are the same person."

Her mouth falls open, and then I proceed to tell her everything.

"I don't know how I'm supposed to ever do this again," I say when I'm finished my story. "I don't know how I can put myself out there and take the risk of loving someone, knowing it could end up breaking me." I look up from my clasped hands. "How do normal, healthy people do it? How do you love without letting it crush you?"

"I don't know," Isabelle says slowly. "I guess … I do get hurt sometimes. And it does feel like I've been crushed. But there's enough love from other people to help me pick myself up and carry on, so over time I realise I haven't been crushed after all. I think that's the key," she says, looking out my window with a thoughtful expression. "You can't just have one person who's your absolute everything. If they hurt you, then you have nothing left. But I have my parents and my brother and my friends—and God. Like a safety net, you know?"

"God," I murmur. "Still pondering that one."

She returns her gaze to me. "So maybe that's what happened with you and Braden. The closer you got to him, the further away you moved from everyone else. You were so completely wrapped up in him and his issues that once he was gone, you had no one else. I mean, that's not actually the way it was. We were all here for you, but you were already so distant that it was almost impossible for us to help you. And your solution to that was to *remain* distant from everyone so no one could ever hurt you again, when you should have been doing the opposite." She pokes me lightly with her toe. "You know?"

"Yeah, I guess. But it's an effort to get close to people."

"Well, it is *now*, because you've pushed so many people away. But it wasn't always, was it?"

I stare across the room at my art-covered walls and push my mind far, far, far back to a time before Braden. To a time before Julia ran away from home. To a time when I couldn't wait to get to school every day to see my friends, and Friday night youth group was a highlight, and my art was vibrant and happy, and smiling was easy.

"You have to start somewhere," Isabelle adds, "so why not start right now?"

"Right now?"

"This afternoon. Come with me to Corner Cafe. Remember the youth group you used to belong to years ago? Most of us are meeting there for a little Christmas celebration."

"What is the point," I say with a sigh, "in getting to know people who are going to be leaving in a few weeks to start university in some other part of the country?"

"Firstly, not everyone is leaving. And secondly, the point is to get out and have fun and chat to people and just … live."

"You kinda sound like Caleb."

Isabelle smiles. "I like that guy."

I shake my head, but I'm smiling. "So … when you say 'right now,' you mean *right now*?"

"Yep, I mean right now. Get some shoes on and let's go."

Part of me still wants to resist, but I know I can't keep doing this. The longer I remain alone, the more miserable I'll end up—not the other way around, despite the lies I've been telling myself over the past year. "Okay," I say eventually.

Isabelle keeps her eyes on me while I grab shoes and a purse, as I if might perform a disappearing act if she looks away for even a second. "I'll meet you outside," I say as we head downstairs. "Just gonna let my mom know I'm going out."

I find Mom at the kitchen table going through her menu for Christmas lunch tomorrow, probably making sure she hasn't forgotten anything. Everyone else has gone for a late afternoon stroll along the promenade. "Mom?" I say, leaning into the kitchen.

She looks up. "Sophie," she says with a smile. "So nice to see you out of your room." Her words hold no sarcasm.

"I'm going out with Isabelle for a bit," I tell her.

"Oh, how nice. You've been working so hard. It's about time you took a break."

Perhaps it is. "Um, I probably won't be home late."

"Okay, sure. Oh, Soph," she adds. "I meant to tell you earlier. We got a new Christmas card. From, uh, Caleb."

Blood rushes into my ears, hammering loudly, and my body seems cold and hot at the same time. My eyes go to the side of the fridge, where I notice a new addition to the Christmas card collection: a white card with a simple outline of an angel and the words 'Happy Christmas' written below it.

Mom stands and comes towards me. "He included a letter with the card. Addressed to me. It was an apology for … well, for what happened with the two of you on the night of the wedding."

I nod slowly, unsure of what to say, wondering if Caleb apologised because he regrets that night or simply because he's sorry he upset my mother.

Mom gives me a small smile. "He's a good guy, actually. A decent young man. I do like him. I was just a bit shocked to, uh, to find him sharing a bed with my youngest daughter."

"Nothing happened, Mom. I told you that already." And it's driving a knife into my heart to think of that evening. Of our kisses and his smile and his arms wrapped around me.

"I know, I know," Mom says. "Not that that's an excuse for the two of you sharing a bed. It still wasn't appropriate. But my first thought was that he was taking advantage of you—which is why I brought up the age difference—but you made it clear that that wasn't the case. And I understand now that the two of you have actually been friends for a long time, so … well, I assume it wasn't just over the space of a few days that you grew close." Her face is pinker than normal, and I wonder if this conversation feels as awkward to her as it does to me. "What I'm trying to say," she continues, "is that if you have feelings for Caleb, I'm not going to stand in the way of that. I certainly don't want to forbid you from loving someone. But I want you to tell me what's going on. I don't want there to be secrets or sneaking about—not that that's possible if he's in a different country, but … I just want to know what's going on, okay?"

I take a deep breath. "We're not—there's nothing—we … had a bit of a falling out." I roll my eyes in an attempt to make it seem less of a big deal than it was. "My fault, of course. Like you said, he's the first guy since Braden, so … Anyway, I totally messed things up."

"Oh, I'm so sorry to hear that," she says, her face falling. And she does sound genuinely sorry. "Do you want to talk about—"

"No. Thank you. It's … I'm on my way out now."

"Sophie." Mom catches my wrist as I turn to leave. She rubs her hand up and down my arm a few times. "What about later? We haven't talked—*really* talked—in a long time. You can tell me about Caleb, and all the projects you're busy with, and how things are working out with your business plan." She chuckles and gives a brief shake of her head. "It still sounds odd to use the words 'business plan' in connection with my eighteen-year-old daughter who only just left school."

I hesitate, breathing in deeply to keep back the tears. She's right that we haven't spoken about anything real or serious in a long time. And Isabelle's words about a safety net keep coming back to me. I remember that Mom is supposed to be part of that safety net—if I'll let her. So I nod. "Okay. That would be nice."

Slowly over the next few weeks, once the wedding and Christmas are far behind us and the overseas family members have returned to their various parts of the world, I start talking to Mom again. About everything. I talk to Sarah, living happily with her new husband a few suburbs away, and to Julia, via Skype. I talk to Isabelle as well, and the new friends I'm starting to make. It's an effort at first, like ticking an item off my to-do list, but it gradually becomes easier. More natural.

And then one day, I come up with the crazy notion that I need to speak to Braden's mother. I'm still haunted by the fact that she blames me, and I need to find a way to get past that. I may be living more of a normal life these days, but it will never be entirely normal with that guilt hanging over me.

Terror grips me as I stand in front of Sharon's house on

a sunny Tuesday morning. Her driveway gate is open—probably broken again—so I force myself to walk right up to the front door. My hand shakes as I clench it into a fist and knock.

She pulls the door open, a frown already in place. "What are you doing here, Sophie?"

"I just want to talk to you. We never actually had a proper conversation after … after Braden's death, and I think it would be good for us."

"I don't see how a proper conversation is going to help anyone," she says.

"Please, Sharon." She might not need this, but I do.

With a sigh, she steps aside and lets me in. I follow her to the lounge, where we sit opposite one another. "Well?" she says.

I waste no time getting to the point. "Maybe I'm wrong, but I feel as though you blame me in part for Braden's suicide."

The way she looks down and presses her lips together without saying anything tells me I'm not wrong. I try not to let that crush me. "It's true," she says eventually. "I do think you were partly responsible for exacerbating the issues that led Braden to his death. You were both too young to be in such a serious relationship. I told him that over and over, and sometimes, when he was in his right mind, he even agreed with me.

"But, Sharon," I say as carefully as I can. "There were issues before Braden and I started dating. It wasn't our relationship that made him that way."

"I was aware there were issues. Of course I was. Do you think I didn't know my son at all? I did, and that's why I was anxious about him dating."

"But … I don't understand." I edge forward a little on the couch. "Were you going to try to keep him from being with someone forever?"

"I—I don't know." Sharon looks away. "It's just— teenagers, with all those volatile emotions rushing around. I knew it would only make him worse. And it did. The two of you together made him worse."

My eyes begin to ache with unshed tears. This isn't how this meeting was supposed to go. We were supposed to get away from blame. We were supposed to understand each other, forgive each other.

"The thing is, Sharon," I say in a wobbly voice. I clear my throat and continue. "I don't think I made him worse. I did everything I could. To draw him out of his pain. To make him happy. To get him to be part of the world. And all those times he broke up with me, I respected that, even though it hurt more than anything. If he didn't want to be with me, then I wasn't going to force him. But he kept coming back to me. I was never the one who initiated getting back together. It was always him."

"You should have said no, Sophie. You knew he wasn't better when he was with you."

"But he was. That's why I thought I was the right person for him. That's why I thought I could really make a difference in his life."

"Well clearly you couldn't," she says tightly. "Because

238

look where your relationship got him."

I bite my lip before forcing myself to say the things I know I need to say. The things I came here to say. The things I know in my heart are the *real* truth. "Braden didn't end his life because of me. There were issues that went much deeper than our relationship. He wasn't a happy person, and no one—not me or you or anyone else in his life—could make him happy." I slowly rise to my feet. "I … I'm so sorry, Sharon." And I really am. She's in terrible pain, and I know she's only blaming me because it's easier to think that things might have turned out differently if I'd never been part of the equation. "I'm sorry," I say again, and then I leave.

I stand on her front steps for a few moments and breathe. The ache inside me isn't gone. If anything, I hurt more deeply now than when I knocked on this door, because I know that nothing has changed between Braden's mother and me. I know she still blames me.

But I'm not utterly crushed. The world isn't collapsing in on me. And even if I'm falling right now, it's okay. I know my safety net will catch me before I hit the bottom.

"HEY!" ISABELLE WAVES ME OVER AS I ENTER CORNER Cafe. "How'd it go with Braden's mom?" she asks as I join her, Lauren and Mark.

"Um ... not so great."

"Ugh, sorry," Isabelle says, taking my hand and squeezing it.

"But I said what I went there to say," I add. "And I think it helped. I felt like crap when I left, but I'm already feeling lighter."

"Well done," Lauren says. "That took serious guts."

"Oh, hey, your new tattoo," Mark says, his eyes lighting up as he reaches across the table for my hand. "When did you get that done?"

"Last week," I tell him as I look down at the new pattern. The single star has become a trail of stars shooting across the base of my thumb.

"It's so pretty," Isabelle says, probably for the tenth time.

"Yeah," I say, a hint of a smile pulling my lips up. I took a bad memory and turned it into a happy one. That single star reminded me of Braden and of being alone, but the star trail reminds me of light and wishes and dreams coming true and never being alone ever again.

I pull my iPad out and order a drink as Isabelle, Lauren and Mark get back to work on … I don't know. Whatever it is they're learning in their theology courses. I don't have any courses to keep up with, but when they meet on Tuesday and Thursday afternoons to work together, I do my email checking and social media updates. I lean back and read the newest email in my inbox.

Hi Angel Artist

I saw your work featured on Clockwork Art yesterday and I LOVE it! I was even more excited when I clicked through to your website and see you do custom work. I need fantasy artwork for 5 book covers. When will you be able to fit me in? I can pay the 50% deposit now for all of them. If there are no slots in your schedule during the next three months, could you pass on recommendations for another artist?

"*Five* book covers?" I say out loud.

"What's that?" Isabelle asks, looking up from her laptop. I show her the email. "Wow. That's a good thing, right? I mean, you're always looking to fill up your schedule with new clients."

"Yes, this is *very* good."

"I saw the feature," Isabelle tells me. "I followed the link you shared on Facebook. There were *tons* of comments on that Clockwork Art page for your work."

"Yeah, it's been amazing. This email about the five book covers isn't the first query I've received based on yesterday's feature."

"That's awesome, Soph."

"You'll have to start using your real name now that you're going professional and all that," Mark says.

"I do, but some of my social profiles still have the word 'angel' in my username, so people still seem to call me that."

Isabelle twists a strand of hair around her finger. "Did you, uh, see that Caleb commented on the feature?"

"What? No. What did he say?" Without waiting for her answer, I'm already opening a new browser tab on my iPad and navigating to the Clockwork Art webpage. I scroll down past my highly detailed steampunk poster and start skimming through the comments.

"It was somewhere near the top," Isabelle says. "One of the first."

I find it a few seconds later.

Way to go, Ash :) It turned out brilliantly. Proud of you.

I start crying.

"What? No!" Isabelle exclaims. "You're not supposed to cry over this."

I shake my head and wipe beneath my eyes as my lips tremble. I haven't heard a single thing from Caleb since the day he walked away from me on the side of the road. I thought he probably hated me. So to hear that he's proud of me instead? "I—I'm fine," I manage to stammer. "Really, I am."

"Are you going to reply to him?" Lauren asks, pushing her textbooks aside and scooting a little closer. I notice that Mark is choosing to remain silent for now. Probably because there's a crying girl involved.

"Yes, I'm just … just thinking of what to say."

"Don't think too hard," Isabelle suggests. "Just say what comes to mind."

"Okay." I type quickly, before I can change my mind.

Thank you :) That means a lot to me.

I lean back in my chair. "Do you think he could ever forgive me for hurting him?"

Isabelle places her elbow on the table and rests her chin in her palm as she examines me. "Why? Do you think you made a mistake letting him go?"

I give her a sad smile. "I undoubtedly made a mistake letting him go. And now he's probably in some distant exotic country falling in love with someone else."

"He's in Canada, actually," Isabelle says. "And he's still single."

"And you know this because …"

"We're friends on Facebook," she explains. "What?" she adds when I give her my 'Seriously' look. "He's a friendly guy. He added me ages ago when we met just before the wedding."

Huh. He didn't add *me*. Or maybe he did, but because I hardly ever use Facebook, his friend request ended up hidden amongst other friend requests. I bite my lip and stare at my reply—**Thank you :) That means a lot to me**—and wonder if he'll possibly know just how much his words mean to me.

WE DON'T START MESSAGING AGAIN, BUT WE DO BEGIN leaving comments on each other's images on Artster. I never used that function much before. I used to 'like' people's artworks and chat to Lex in the private messages section of the app, and that was about it. But now we comment on each other's art all the time. And just so it doesn't look too weird, I make the effort to leave comments on other artist's uploads as well.

I keep waiting for the day when Lex—Caleb—sends a private message, reopening that line of communication between us, but it doesn't come. Perhaps he thinks it's safer this way. Comments are public. There's no baring of one's soul. No chance to have one's heart broken. I don't blame him for wanting to protect himself. Instead, I'm grateful for every single comment he leaves on my paintings. I write careful and thoughtful comments on his pictures, and I upload more art than ever these days, just so I can see another comment pop up from him.

And then, one day, an advert shows up on Facebook for VAU Art Con in Rome in March. That silly thing Caleb and I ended up fighting over. That thing he will almost certainly be at. I check my savings account, even though I've known for a while that I have enough money to begin travelling. I just haven't known where to begin—and once I started hanging out with Isabelle a little more and making a few actual friends, I found that I quite enjoyed being at home still.

But perhaps the time has come to make a move. And this art con, where I will no doubt learn a huge amount of valuable information, could be the place to begin. And, let's be honest, there's the possibility of Caleb. Right now, that's of more interest to me than anything else.

But what if he isn't there?

Or what if he is, but he doesn't actually want to see me?

Or what if he doesn't mind seeing me, but he thinks of me as little more than an acquaintance these days?

Well that's a risk you have to take if you want to be a human being living in this world.

The memory of Caleb's words make me smile, but it's a sad smile when I remember my response to him. I basically told him he wasn't worth the risk.

Now I have to show him that he is.

IT'S AN ODD FEELING, STEPPING ONTO LAND IN ANOTHER country and knowing that it's the other side of the world, yet the ground still feels exactly like the ground at home. I haven't travelled nearly enough yet to have become used to it. And Caleb was right—of course—about travelling alone. The moment I first catch sight of St. Peter's Basilica, I'm so overcome with excitement that I want to grab the nearest person and point it out to them. It's so much less fun not having someone to share that excitement with.

When I've finally navigated various forms of public transport and found the bed and breakfast apartment I'm staying in, I collapse onto the bed. The tiny room is nice enough, and I can't help falling asleep almost immediately. I remain asleep for most of my first day, making up for having been awake the whole way through the two flights here.

I wake early on the first day of the con. I walk along the streets, breathing in the cool air, listening to the foreign language, and marvelling at the fact that I'm actually *in Rome*—and building up a good deal of nervous anticipation at the thought of maybe, possibly, finally seeing Caleb. I know he's here. Isabelle saw something recently on his Facebook page about him leaving for Italy soon. I didn't tell him I decided to come. My fear that he might say he doesn't want to see me kept me from sending a message to him. Now that I'm here, I try not to think how much worse it will be if he says the same thing to my face.

Thanks to the maps app on my phone, it's fairly easy for me to find the art con venue. It's only once I'm inside, overwhelmed by the displays and the panels and the live art, that I think about the fact that I'm going to have to actually contact Caleb if I have any hope of meeting up with him here. I wander around, trying to work up the courage to send him a message. I read the sign pointing to the exhibitions on the next level up, and I'm surprised and excited to see the name of the woman who does the body painting. The woman whose work Caleb and I were trying to mimic when we played around in my garage. After seeing the word 'live' next to her name, I hurry up the stairs.

I find a large crowd around her section, hundreds of people gathered to watch her as she paints two men sitting on a couch. She's also in the process of the painting the actual couch, as well as the floor and the walls and everything else around the men. It's fascinating watching the three dimensional scene appear to lose its depths and become two dimensional. My gaze travels across the crowd as I watch people's reactions—

—and then I see him.

My stomach does a somersault at the sight of Caleb near the front on the far side of the crowd. I don't stop to think. I jump up and down. I wave and shout his name, which, fortunately, doesn't appear to disturb anybody. There's so much chattering and noise going on in this place that one more shouting girl doesn't make much difference.

I know the moment he sees me because that smile I love so much lights up his face. I turn and push through the crowd. I hurry around the outside, never losing sight of him as he weaves through the crowd. When he finally breaks free and looks around for me, I run towards him. It's instinctive, and I don't stop to wonder what might happen if he doesn't actually want me flinging my arms around him.

We collide. His arms tighten around me, so strong and secure, and he's laughing into my hair, and then he's kissing me everywhere. My lips, my cheeks, my hair, my ears. "I can't believe how much I missed you," he says between kisses. "And I can't believe you're here. And—" He takes a breath and steps back. "Is it okay to kiss you?" he asks as an afterthought.

In answer, I take his face in my hands and pull him against me, pressing a fierce and longing kiss to his lips. Then I lean back. "I'm so sorry for how things ended before. I was so stupid. Of course you're worth the risk. I … I just needed some time to sort myself out before I could see that."

His forehead touches mine, and he kisses the tip of my nose. "I would have been happy to give you all the time in the world. And I'm sorry too. I said so many insensitive things after you told me about Braden."

"It's okay, I needed to hear them."

"But I acted as if I didn't care about this horrible tragedy you'd—"

"You didn't act like that. I know you cared. I was the one dealing with it in the wrong way. I kept distancing myself from everyone, trying to keep myself safe, when that was the total opposite of what I should have been doing."

He kisses me again, long and slow this time, and it's all I can do to remember how to stand upright. When he pulls back, I have to blink and catch my breath. "Why didn't you tell me you were coming?" he asks, tucking stray wisps of hair behind my ear.

"I … I wasn't sure you'd want to see me."

He shakes his head, his lips stretching into another smile. "Sophie, I've been wanting to see you since the moment I walked away from you outside that church."

I start laughing as happiness bubbles up inside me, uncontainable. "I feel like I have a zillion things to tell you. All the things I thought of in the past few months and couldn't tell you because I didn't think you'd want to hear from me. And all the things I didn't tell you while we were chatting online during the past two and a bit years, because I didn't feel like you'd want to know those things about me."

"I want to know everything about you, Sophie Henley."

"I kinda want to know everything about you too."

His arms encircle me. "You're in Rome," he says, as if he still can't quite believe it.

My smile is wide. "I'm in Rome."

"Where to next?"

I shrug and give him another kiss. "Wherever you want to go."

VISIT

WWW.TROUBLESERIES.COM

FOR BONUS MATERIAL BASED ON
THE TROUBLE WITH FALLING

AND DON'T MISS OUT ON THE REST OF
THE TROUBLE SERIES!

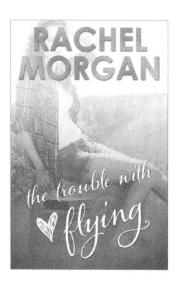

RACHEL MORGAN
the trouble with flying

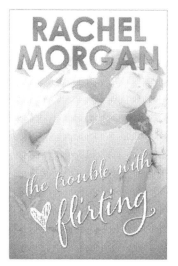

RACHEL MORGAN
the trouble with flirting

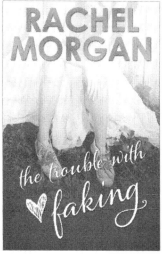

RACHEL MORGAN
the trouble with faking

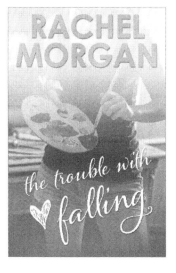

RACHEL MORGAN
the trouble with falling

ACKNOWLEDGEMENTS

Thank you to God, my husband, and my family. for being there to catch me when I was the one falling. I've never been through anything like what Sophie went through, but in those moments when I felt like darkness was all I knew, I was never actually alone.

Thank you to my brother and sister for both having weddings in the same year that I decided to write this book. It was a great reminder of all the planning, the fun, the stress, the family gatherings, and the excitement surrounding a wedding. So convenient of you guys to plan it that way ;-)

Thank you, Alexa Meade, for inspiring the body painting that Sophie and Caleb attempt to do. You have no idea who I am, but I think your art is amazing! Anyone reading these acknowledgements should go check out her work.

I'm also hugely grateful to all the artists whose digital fantasy paintings inspire me, no matter which book I'm working on. I wish I could do what you do.

And thank you to you, my fabulous readers, for waiting so long for this one. Almost two years after the date I intially planned for this book to be published, Sophie's story is finally out there.

© Gavin van Haght

Rachel Morgan spent a good deal of her childhood living
in a fantasy land of her own making, crafting endless stories of
make-believe and occasionally writing some of them down.
After completing a degree in genetics and discovering
she still wasn't grown-up enough for a 'real' job, she decided
to return to those story worlds still spinning around her
imagination. These days she spends much of her time
immersed in fantasy land once more, writing fiction
for young adults and those young at heart.

Rachel lives in Cape Town with her husband and
three miniature dachshunds. She is the author of the
bestselling Creepy Hollow series and the sweet
contemporary romance Trouble series.

www.rachel-morgan.com

50644738R00162

Made in the USA
San Bernardino, CA
29 June 2017